It had been forty-eight hours since I'd slept.

Five days since I'd started playing cat and mouse with crazed, supernatural killer Rafe Stevens.

Almost a week since he'd entered my dreams.

"He can't get you," Dan swore. "Please. Trust me."

Trust had been a tenuous thing between us, but I'd asked him to have faith in me. Now I had to do the same.

Looking into his blue eyes, I took a leap of faith and jumped into the abyss.

TERRI CLARK

Sleepless

HARPER TEEN

An Imprint of HarperCollins*Publishers*

HarperTeen is an imprint of
HarperCollins Publishers.

Library of Congress catalog card number: 2007940007
ISBN 978-0-06-137596-5

Typography by Andrea Vandergrift

First Edition

For Dan, Jeremy, and Casey
You are my dream come true.

ACKNOWLEDGMENTS

So many people have helped me realize my dream. Lexa Hillyer, Cori Deyoe, Kristin Marang, Caren Johnson, Kari Sutherland, and Gretchen Hirsch. Thank you for seeing the potential in me and for guiding me along the way.

Thank you to all of my family and friends for believing in me, especially my mom, who gave me her strength of spirit and passion for reading. I'm truly blessed to be surrounded by so much love and support.

My biggest thank-you goes to my own hero, Dan, and my two children, Jeremy and Casey. Because of you I know "happily ever after" is a reality.

Hugs to everyone at the Smoky Hill Library. You're an amazing group and you've bettered my life. Thank you for your camaraderie, inspiration, and encouragement.

Last, but never least, eternal gratitude to my best friend, Lynda Sandoval. You're always there for the good, the bad, and the ugly. I'd never have made it down this long road without you. Your friendship is a gift I'll always treasure.

"Who's to say that dreams and nightmares aren't as real as the here and now?"
—John Lennon

Sleepless

Chapter 1

"When are you going to hook up with a hottie?"

I spat out a gulp of Mocha Frappuccino in a movie-worthy spit take and gave my best friend, Coral, a censuring glare. She merely laughed and arched an insistent "answer me" eyebrow.

"Sheesh, Coral," I whined, wiping mocha off my bare legs. "Give a girl some warning before you ax her with a question like that."

She took an exaggerated slurp of iced green tea before saying, "Not a chance, Trinity. You're too smooth at avoidance and misdirection, so I have to catch you off guard. Besides"—she pointed to a spot of melting frap that I'd missed on my bare stomach—"the look on your face was priceless. I only wish I'd caught it on camera."

I rolled my eyes, just imagining her posting my blooper on YouTube. Like people didn't think I was enough of a freak already. Feeling dry, but sticky, I settled back into my lounge chair. We were chillin' out on SoBe in our new bikinis, mine a ruby red with crossbones, hers bubble-gum pink with lime-green polka dots. No doubt we looked luscious, but you couldn't call us your average sun worshippers. Not when we were reclining under an oversized umbrella to protect our skin. Me, because I don't do tan, and Coral, because her fair, freck-led skin burns from the slightest rays.

I dug a hole in the sand and tucked my drink into it, then rooted around in my tattoo sling bag for my bottle of Midnight Marauder nail polish. Lavishing my toes with attention I painted them black and avoided Coral's per-sistent gaze. "What do you expect me to do?" I asked her. "Pounce on the first guy who walks by?"

Coral gave an inelegant snort, stifling any

follow-ups with her hand. I looked up to see what had caused her reaction and shuddered as a fleshy man in a too-tight Speedo strutted by with an impressive amount of confidence—no doubt, a Florida tourist. When we caught sight of his back we both squealed, "Ew!" simultaneously and collapsed onto each other in a fit of giggles. He glowered at us.

"Poor man," Coral whispered, once she regained her composure. "He really should get lasered."

"Imagine the smell of burnt hair," I said and twitched my nose.

"Ack, stop." She puffed out her cheeks like she had to vomit. "Now I'm twice as traumatized."

I grinned and wiggled my nearly dry toes, but just as I let my guard down she swooped in again.

"I'm not letting up on you." She swung her legs over the side of her chair, facing me. Her eyes were alight with her usual energy and exuberance. Admittedly, I loved her contagious enthusiasm, but not when she meant to

3

back me into a corner.

I gave her my typical "here we go again" groan.

She responded by slapping my leg.

"Hey!"

"This is our last summer before college," she said, ignoring my yelp. "We're supposed to live it up! Expand our personal boundaries. Be adventurous. Discover who we are."

She outstretched her arms and I held up a warning finger. "If you start singing 'Breaking Free,' there's going to be bloodshed."

Coral smirked. "Apropos—but I was going for 'Unwritten.'"

"A better choice," I conceded. Lord knows I'd take Natasha Bedingfield over *High School Musical* any day. "But save the solo. I get your point. Summer equals freedom."

"No!" Coral shouted. "It's more than that. Here it is, July seventh, and classes start on August twenty-seventh. It's going fast! This should be a summer of change. Of metamorphosis. Of transmogrification."

"Great, now you're going all Harry Potter

on me," I mumbled. "I'm not morphing into a cat."

"That's not what I meant. We"—she waved a finger between the two of us—"can be who-ever we want. We're not tied to the labels we were given in high school."

"You mean Goth Girl and Soccer Star?" I shot a glance from my piratical swimsuit to the soccer ball under her chair. "Gee, so much has changed," I sneered.

Coral blew out an exasperated breath. "I don't mean that. Will you listen?"

I folded my arms over my chest and locked my gaze on her. "Undivided attention."

"Thank you," she said. "I'm not talking about the core things that make us . . . well, *us*. Yes, you're Goth Girl and I'm Soccer Star, but we're more than that."

"Here it comes," I interrupted and then bit my lip when she motioned for me to zip my mouth.

"I'm klutzy and clueless," she admitted.

"You're comical and naïve," I defended.

She pointed to a bevy of bruises on her legs.

"Connect the dots, babe," she told me.

"Fine," I said, "so you're klutzy. It's part of your charm."

She smiled at me, grasping my hand. "I know you love me just the way I am, Trin. You're my best friend. But I *would* like to be a little more poised and I hate feeling like I'm always missing the punch line." She let go of me and shrugged. "I've always been too sheltered and you"—she gave me a sad smile, not a piteous one, but a compassionate one—"you've seen too much."

I opened my mouth to object, thinking she wasn't nearly as naïve as she believed, but she spoke before I could.

"There's a part of you I don't even know," she said softly.

I lowered my eyes, unable to deny it. Still, after all these years, unable to explain.

"It's okay," she said. "I know enough about you to be sure of one thing. You take too much of the world on your shoulders and you don't allow yourself to *be*."

Be? It sounded like such a simple word.

"You hold back, Trin. You hide. I don't know why, but you're like a turtle. Your shell protects you and keeps you hidden. When are you going to peek your head out?"

When indeed? I didn't know how to answer, couldn't . . .

Being the smart chick she is, Coral quickly realized her point had hit home and she snapped back to her bubbly self so as not to push me too far. "You know what we're going to do this summer?"

"Uh"—I scrunched up my face as if in heavy concentration—"you're going to soccer camp and I'm going to wallow in loneliness?"

"You're only half right," she chirped.

I flinched at her perkiness and asked myself a question I'd asked a thousand times. How had I, dark and dreary, become best friends with her, sunlight and rainbows? Oh, yeah. Fifth-grade Girl Scouts. I'd misheard my mom and thought she'd enrolled me in *ghoul* scouts. To my utter disappointment it had been all badges and trefoils, not bats and zombies. Fortunately, when I burst into tears someone came to my

7

rescue with a tissue and a Thin Mint—Coral. Despite being polar opposites, she and I had been inseparable ever since. We were like frickin' Eeyore and Tigger.

Until now. She was bouncing away for the summer.

"'Tis true I'm going to soccer camp, but I'm making it my goal to experience new things. Like in *Sisterhood of the Traveling Pants*."

I gasped. "You're going to lose your virginity to your soccer coach?"

"No! Well, maybe." She grinned and waggled her eyebrows. "Depends how hot he is."

"Coral!" I shrieked in outrage. "What's gotten into you?"

"Nothing. Yet."

I groaned and covered my ears.

She yanked my hands down. "Okay, all kidding aside. This isn't about 'losing it' before college. But when I come back from camp I want to be a new person. I'm making it my goal to get a little wilder. Get a little wiser."

"'Get down tonight,'" I sang.

Coral threw her copy of *Glamour* magazine

at me. "I'm serious here," she hissed.

I held up my hands in surrender, laughing. "Okay, I get it. You're serious. You're coming back more . . . experienced."

"Exactly. Not necessarily sexually, but definitely more mature. I don't intend to have that wide-eyed, greenhorn, college freshman"—she smacked her forefinger and thumb into an L on her forehead—"loser look on my face when we get to UM."

"Hey!" I pinched her knee. "I resemble that remark."

"Chances are we both will, no matter what we do this summer, but that's not the point," she insisted.

I took a sip of my drink. "And the point is?"

"Discovery," she said, as if the answer was obvious. "Growth. Finding out just who we are."

I smirked. "You sound like a coming-of-age novel."

Her eyes widened. "That's right. That's what this is. Our coming-of-age novel, and like the song says, 'Today is where your book begins. The rest is still unwritten.'"

I shook my head, amused by her *tabula rasa* attitude. "I think mine would read more like a horror story."

"Well, there's always blood, sex, and rock and roll in those, so it couldn't be all bad," she said jokingly. "Seriously, you can change things, whatever those things are, but you need to start by getting out more this summer. By living!"

"Come on," I grumbled. "I'm here, aren't I?" I waved my hand around the glorious beach surrounding us. "It's not like I'm agoraphobic."

"No," she agreed, "but you don't date. You don't go to parties, unless I drag your ass along and then I usually have to resort to blackmail or bribery and if I'm real honest—"

"Like you'd be anything else!"

"You really, really need to lighten up."

"Hmph," I sniffed. "I take offense at that. Did I not just laugh my butt off at Mr. Wereback?"

"Yeah, but there's lots of times where you

act all emo"—she mocked one of my contemplative, semi-dejected looks—"and it wouldn't hurt you to wear some bright colors on occasion."

"Hullo!" I pointed to my bikini. "Red is bright."

"So is blue," she argued. "I'd love to see you in a baby blue that matches your eyes. With your black hair you'd look gorgy. I'm not saying you can't keep your Goth-rock style. It's you, and I love it. But you could dress it up sometimes."

I heaved a sigh. Was she right? Was I too stark? "Blue?" I asked uncertainly.

"Blue," she said emphatically.

"'Kay," I agreed. It seemed a small enough thing to do. "I can try that."

"Yes!" She beamed like I'd just offered her a winning Lotto ticket. "Since you're so agreeable, I have another homework assignment for you while I'm gone."

I shook my head. "Oh, no. You can't be serious. It's summer. I don't do homework. Plus I just conceded a point to you."

"You can do this, too. You are required—"

"By what law?" I sassed.

"By the law vested in me"—she thumped herself on the chest—"your best friend. As I was saying, before I was so rudely interrupted, you are required to spread your wings and soar while I'm gone." She lifted her arms and flapped them slowly like large wings.

I cocked my thumb and forefinger, aimed at her, and pretended to pull the trigger. "And how am I supposed to do that when you aren't here to pitch me over the cliff?"

She leaped out of her chair. "Jump!"

I snorted. "You make it sound so easy."

"It is." She sat on the edge of my chair. "You just have to put your mind to it. Buy a new—blue—dress. Go to a party. I know Mariah's annual birthday bash is next month. And here's the biggest requirement for an A. Go on a date."

"Right," I scoffed. "No one asked me out in high school. Why would they now?"

"Who says they have to ask you?"

When I opened my mouth to object she

spoke fast to stop me.

"You're the master of your destiny, Trin. Create your own path. You can do it. You can—"

"All right, all right, Confucius."

"Is that a yes?" she asked excitedly.

"Yes," I said. Anything to shut her up.

"Yes, what?" she insisted.

Drat. So much for being vague. "Yes, I'll make an effort to 'spread my wings.'"

"And?"

"And"—I clenched my teeth—"I'll buy a frickin' *blue* dress."

"And?"

"Corrr-al," I warned.

"And?" she persisted.

"And I'll get out more."

"On a . . ." she led.

"On a date," I barked. "Happy now?"

"Not until you pinkie promise. And no crossies."

My jaw dropped. "We haven't done that since grade school!"

"Still," she said earnestly. "This is too

important. I need to know you'll do what you say. I know you'd never break a pinkie promise."

Shit! There was no backing out now. I clenched my fist for a moment and then popped out my pinkie. Coral wrapped hers around mine and we went through an intricate pattern of hand motions ending in a double fist bump.

Satisfied, Coral flopped back into her chair with a sigh. "Now I won't worry about you while I'm gone."

"Great," I muttered.

"And, just so you know, I'll be checking in."

"*Ter*-rific."

"Oh, come on." She gave my shoulder a playful shove. "Don't be mad, I just worry about you."

"I know," I said. How could I be mad at her for that?

"Trinity," she said, her voice dipping low and soft. "I know things haven't been easy. Especially in the last year." She studied me closely before

14

blurting, "Your mom told me about this morning's article."

I closed my eyes.

And there it was.

The real reason for this trip and my summer "homework."

"So Mom put you up to this *beach day*?"

"Not exactly," Coral hedged.

I gave her a doubtful glare.

"Well, I called and said I wanted to do something today. She mentioned the article and suggested I drive us up here. She knows how much you love the beach."

I nodded. Again, I couldn't be surprised or angry.

"The bastard should've gone to jail," she said quietly.

"Yeah," I said wearily. "He should have."

"But it's not your fault, Trin. It's just not."

Wasn't it?

I'd dreamed about Kiri Delai more than a year ago. It was Wednesday, June sixth, one day after her parents reported her missing.

In my dream we straddled two surfboards, bobbing lazily in the Atlantic. Dark clouds churned above and the air crackled with dangerous energy. She wore denim capris, a black sash belt that matched her tank top, and beaded flip-flops, which dangled from her toes under the clear cerulean surface. The impracticality of her outfit in the water didn't faze me—I'd learned to accept bizarre inconsistencies in my visions—but she had an odd *glow* about her I'd never seen before. She seemed to shimmer like sparkles on the water, an ethereal soul in a distorted dreamscape.

"You don't 'member me, do you?" she asked with an adorable, impish grin.

The dimple in her right cheek struck a note of familiarity, but I couldn't immediately place her. She flung her wavy black hair behind her shoulder and looked at me with innocent, chocolate-brown eyes. "Surf camp."

Oh, *right*! Last summer, when Mom was feeling adventurous, she'd dragged me off to

Cocoa Beach for a week's worth of family surf lessons. (That would explain the coastal backdrop of my dream.) Three other families had been in our group. This girl, I think she'd been in sixth grade at the time, was there with her parents. Small world that it is, we found out they lived in Nevaeh, the same town we did. Immediately, Kiri won over everyone's hearts with her perky personality and contagious smile.

She was the kind of girl I'd always secretly wished I could be—carefree, vivacious, and spirited. A lot like Coral.

"Kiri! The Polynesian Princess," I said, fondly remembering my nickname for her. "Boy, you grew up a lot in a year."

"Thanks!" she said excitedly. "I see you're still working the whole dark beauty angle. Very Amy Lee. It works for you."

I grimaced. My black hair and light blue eyes occasionally drew comparisons to the Evanescence singer, but I made a conscientious effort *not* to stand out.

"Thanks," I said anyhow. "And, of course, I

remember you. We only wiped out on our boards together, like—"

"A million times," she interjected.

I winced in empathy. "Yeah, but we got better," I reminded her.

"Definitely," she agreed. "It was a summer to remember."

I nodded and let the warm memory soak in—but then sudden suspicion interrupted me. This wasn't just a pleasant walk down memory beach. There was something more. . . .

"What are you doing here, Kiri?"

She heaved a weighty sigh.

"I didn't wanna come. Didn't wanna bother you. But . . ."

"But?" I asked, my nerves pulled taut.

"You gotta find me soon," she whispered, her eyes filled with tears and terror. "Or he'll kill me. . . ."

My stomach plummeted to the depths of the ocean and I trembled.

If only I hadn't been too late.

If only I could've saved her.

If only my nightmares had died with her.

* * *

"Trin?"

I looked at Coral, having forgotten for a moment that I was on a real beach with my best friend and not the ghost of a dead girl.

"You okay?"

"Yeah, yeah," I said, not really sure. "Just a little overheated, I think."

"Wanna go?" she asked, brow pinched with worry.

"Why don't we?"

"Hey, if I—"

"It's not you." I softened my interruption with a smile. "Promise."

"'Kay." She returned my smile. "Then let's blow this umbrella stand and go get some ice cream."

"Cheesecake with peanut butter cups?" I asked, licking my lips.

"In a chocolate-dipped waffle cone," Coral added.

My mouth watered and for a moment I decided to let myself ignore all the reasons why I could never really be a normal teenager.

For most people dreams are nonsensical fantasies.

For me dreams are an intrusive, ugly reality.

And though I thought my worst nightmare had already happened, it was just about to begin.

Chapter 2

*E*ver heard of lucid dreaming?

It's when you're aware you're dreaming while inside your dream. Like, you're in the middle of some totally nonsensical illusion and your dream-self says, "This is stupid. Wake up!"

It's kinda trippy, really.

Everyone does it subconsciously, on occasion.

Quacky New Agers even "practice" it by making a conscientious effort before they go to sleep to maintain their cognizance. The idea is they'll somehow achieve divine insight and wisdom by having a waking awareness in their dreams.

Whatever.

But me? I've never dreamed any other way. *Ever*.

No showing-up-naked-for-school nightmares or missing-an-exam dreams for me. I don't even get to enjoy lusty fantasies about Jensen Ackles or my secret crushes. Nope. I dream about real places, real people, real events, and I'm *always* aware that I'm dreaming. It's been that way since I was seven. My mom first noticed my prescience after my dad died. She thinks losing him shocked my system so bad that it "awakened" this—I hate the *words*: gift, ability, and power; it's more like an *aberration*. Anyhow, according to Mom, shamans call my skill *dream walking*. Is that woo-woo, or what? Call it what you like, it's completely complicated my life. Sometimes I'll even meet people in my dreams right before I meet them in real life. Inevitably, I end up with this awkward sense of "Don't I know you?" until I remember, "*Oh, yeah*. Dream." Not cool. It's not like I can say, "That's riiiight. I met you last night. In my sleep."

Think it sounds like I've got some sort of

tight superpower? Trust me, *it's bogus*.

I see things I don't want to see, meet people I'd rather not know exist, and hear things that make me feel way older than eighteen and not in a cool, "I'm so mature" way.

Worst of all, this anomaly makes me feel different. Abnormal. Freaky.

But what can I do? Quit sleeping? *Come on, Trinity. Give it up cold turkey. Kick the habit. Just say no!* I wish.

So, I dream.

Then I do my best to block out the ugly things I learn—against my will, I might add—within my waking nightmares.

For instance, I learned that cliquey prom queen Belinda Thaniel ices people with bitchiness not to be ultra-cool but to keep people at a safe distance. She doesn't want anyone to know about her meth-addicted-mess-of-a-father.

Come on, how would you deal with knowing that kind of shit?

I don't.

Or rather I didn't.

But each time I learned someone's dark

secret and did nothing to—I don't know—illuminate it, a part of me shriveled up and died. I got harder. Darker. I mean, if you think the media desensitizes you to violence and horrors, try hopping into my head for an episode or two. I've been seeing these bleak snapshots of people's lives for as long as I can remember.

But nothing compared to Kiri.

He murdered her.

And I'd been drowning ever since.

Figuratively, of course, not literally. Although I'd just let myself sink to the bottom of my pool. I'd been trying to swim away my worries. The laps had tired me physically, but mentally my brain still worked like a hamster in a wheel, treading over the same area, not getting anywhere.

Oh, no! Wasn't that the definition of insanity?

Probably I was crazy, but I simply couldn't get Kiri out of my mind.

Or him.

I circled my arms under the water to keep

24

steady and blew out a few air bubbles to watch them rise. Then I braced my toes on the pool floor and catapulted myself to the surface, where I flipped to my back. The water muffled my ears and the warm sun soothed me. Cradled by the water I let myself float into a Zen state.

This was my meditation, my way to globally disconnect and emotionally reconnect. I quieted my soul like this. But it was always short-lived.

"Trin?"

I tried to ignore her, to stay in my zone, but the splash on my face told me she wouldn't be dissuaded.

I opened my eyes and frowned at my mom.

"We need to talk," she said, her voice soft but serious.

"Can't it wait?"

She shook her head and I let my legs sink like the knot in my stomach. I knew what she wanted to talk about and I didn't.

"I'm fine," I told her, ducking my head back to smooth my hair.

25

"I know," she said, "but maybe I'm not."

Aw, hell. I never thought of that.

I love my mom more than anyone else on the planet, and I hated to see her suffer as much as she hated to see me suffer. This—*dream drama*—had taken a toll on her, as well. Maybe more than I realized.

Reluctantly, I swam to the ladder and hoisted myself out of the pool. She met me at the edge and wrapped a towel around me before leading me through our sliding glass door to the kitchen.

I plunked down in one of our dining chairs, pulling up my knees, and cocooned myself in the towel.

"Did you have fun at SoBe?" she asked, much too casually, as she poured me a glass of fresh-squeezed lemonade.

"Yeah." I took a sip of my drink and relished the way my tongue turned inside out from the tartness.

"What did you do?"

She sat across from me, watching me so

intently I started to feel like an amoeba under a microscope.

"Uh"—I shrugged—"the usual."

"You came home awful quiet," she said, her momtenna clearly raised.

I narrowed my eyes. "I thought we were talking about you, not me."

"We are"—her gaze broke from mine and she absently rubbed at the condensation on her glass—"but I, that is"—she puffed out a frustrated breath and then looked at me—"I'm having a hard time since the news hit, so I can only imagine how you must feel."

I sucked a corner of my lip into my mouth and bit it to stave off tears. I refused to cry. Instead I let anger burn away my grief. For months following Kiri's death I'd been incapacitated with grief, and now, weeks after attending her one-year memorial service, I still struggled not to thrust myself down that dark tunnel again.

I decided, instead, to focus on how pissed I was at the *Miami Herald* reporter who'd outted me at the memorial. How could he expose me like that? Last year, police refused to release my name as the "psychic" confidante on the case because of my juvenile status. But now I've been disclosed as the witness because I'm finally eighteen years old and a registered freshman at the University of Miami.

Ever since the media had released my name, every Tom, Dick, and Nutcase had been after me and my dreaming abilities. And today they had blabbed my name again.

So *not* what I needed!

If that wasn't bad enough there was the absolute injustice of the trial. When the sentence hit the news first thing this morning it had been too much to bear. Then, to make things worse, our phone rang off the hook with interview requests. As if!

I just wanted the day to end.

For everything to go away.

"Rafe Stevens is a sick S.O.B., but he's no schizophrenic," I finally snapped. "I mean, 'Asmodai made me do it,' my ass. With a little research and some decent acting skills anyone can pretend to be crazy. And that's exactly what Rafe did. I know it. Kiri's parents know it. And—"

"I know it, too, honey," she interrupted. "There's no doubt in our minds he pretended to be crazy, but it appears Judge McClure thought otherwise."

"Who believes a man who says a lust demon made him do it?"

Mom shrugged. "He must've been convincing, and that psychiatrist, Dr. Erskine, says he suffered from schizophrenia. I'm sure that carried a lot of weight."

Aghast, I asked, "You're not saying you believe Rafe's schizo, are you?"

"No"—she waved her hand in denial—"what I'm saying is, unfortunately, what's done is done."

"Well, it's not fair," I complained. "And please don't tell me 'Life's not fair,' I think I know that."

"Yeah, baby, you do. But he's locked up and that's what matters most."

"In a frickin' psych hospital. I wanted him

to be Big John's bitch," I seethed. "Kiri was thirteen. He strangled her before she could even have her first kiss. Her first boyfriend." Tears stung my eyes and I blinked furiously to stop them.

"It's devastating," she agreed. Scooting her chair around the table, she wrapped her arms around me. "Things will never be the same, but it's finally over."

"It doesn't feel like it," I whispered into her neck.

"Are you dreaming about him?"

I gasped. "How'd you know?"

"I'm your mom."

I pulled away. "I have dreamed about him"—I rubbed my forehead—"but they're not like my usual dreams."

She rested her elbows on the table, braced her chin in her hands, and waited for me to continue.

"I—I think they're nightmares."

"Really?" she asked, clearly as surprised as I had been.

"Yeah, I've thought about it and thought

about it and I don't think they could've been anything else. They weren't lucid dreams. I wasn't even in them."

"So what're they about?"

"I don't know exactly. They're sorta fuzzy. I just *know* it's him."

"I think that's normal considering everything you've been through."

"Mom, I don't want him in my life anymore."

"I know, Trin. You just need some time. The trial's done and Rafe's gone. You can move on. Heal."

"How? If only I'd—"

"You couldn't have done anything more than you did."

"Yeah, right."

"You called her parents as soon as you dreamed about her—"

"I know, but—"

"If it hadn't been for you," Mom said, holding up a finger, "the police wouldn't have found Rafe at the scene and who knows how long it would've been before they found Kiri."

I grimaced at the picture in my mind. "They found her body. Not her."

"Rafe could've gotten away and harmed someone else."

She had a point. Still, I sulked.

"You stopped him, honey." She lowered her hand. "That's way more than anyone could ask of you."

I tucked my forehead on my knees. "How come every time I try to help, things backfire?"

"This didn't backfire. It was physically impossible for you to get help to Kiri any sooner than you did. As for Timmy, I'll say what I always have, you did the right thing."

"He hated me," I cried.

"Both of you were nine. He was scared. He said he hated you out of fear, but confronting him about what you saw in your dream got him out of an abusive situation."

"I made him lose his mom."

"His mom who was *beating* him. How do you know removing Timmy from that situation wasn't the best thing that happened to him? You don't."

I shook my head. "He was placed in foster care."

"So? Maybe a loving family adopted him. I don't know how many times I've wished I could track that child down."

"Don't," I pleaded, scared at what she might find.

After seeing my best friend look at me with black hatred in his eyes as he was taken from his home, I refused to sleep for two days. I didn't want any more dreams.

My poor mom had finally resorted to giving me some cold medicine in a glass of grape juice to help me sleep.

After that, for the most part, I kept people's secrets and kept to myself.

Until Kiri.

And look how that turned out.

Never again . . .

"Sweetheart, you need to quit blaming yourself and start living."

I groaned. "I already heard this speech once today."

"And did it have any effect?"

"I agreed to"—I lifted my arms and flapped them more like a chicken than a soaring eagle—"spread my wings, buy a blue dress, and go on a date."

My mom whistled low. "That girl is good."

"You have no idea," I grumbled.

My mom chuckled and I smiled, despite myself, glad for the respite.

"And Coral leaves tomorrow?"

"Yeah." I sighed. "I don't know how I'll survive."

"It's only for a short while. You'll—"

The doorbell rang.

Mom frowned. "I'll get it."

"Wait!" I hollered, jumping from my chair. "I'm going to my room. No correspondents or crazies allowed. I'll be on my computer."

Upstairs, I aimlessly trolled around MySpace and left a "BFF's Forever" comment on Coral's page. Then I plugged in some headphones and surfed YouTube.

"Trinity," Mom called loud enough for me to hear, "someone's here to see you."

"Mo-om." I yanked off my headset, tilted back in my computer chair, and swung around to face her. "I told you, now that the stupid newserazzi has released my name I don't want to talk to anyone. I refuse to be the next James Van Praagh or some other freak show mediator."

"I'm sorry you're upset." She leaned against the doorframe to my bedroom and smiled with more than a little patience. In her blue jeans and Juicy hoodie she looked less momish than she sounded. "But, come on, Trin. Don't you think I know by now you aren't aspiring to be the next psychic TV star? There isn't another psycho spiritualist at our door. And, besides, didn't I buffer you then? Haven't I *always* protected you from the metaphysical groupies?"

I pulled my bare feet up onto my chair and gave her a sheepish look. "Sorry." It was true, she'd always shielded me the best she could from outside interest, and she'd accepted long ago that I found my "gift" more of a curse than a blessing—even if she did still hope to convince me otherwise. If she could've spared me my dreams she'd have done it in a heartbeat. Shoving my long bangs out of my eyes I peered at her, sans the skepticism, and asked, "So, who is it?"

Mom glanced over her shoulder, down the stairs to whoever stood there. Lowering her voice, she said, "It's Devlin's son."

My jaw dropped and my feet hit the floor. "Devlin? As in, Rafe Stevens's lawyer? No way."

"Way," she said, clearly as shocked as I was.

I shook my head in denial. "I wouldn't want to talk to Devlin. And I sure don't want to talk to his son. Boot him."

"I think you should speak with him." She held up her hand to stop any argument. "Just listen. He . . . well . . . he says he wants to apologize."

"What for? His dad's the slimeball who let Rafe get away with murder!" I exploded.

"Trinity!"

"It's okay, Ms. Michaels," he said from behind her, making us both jump. "She's right."

Eyes squinted, I made some quick observations. I had, of course, seen him in court, but I'd refused to really look at him. I figured he had to be every bit as despicable as his father. Now I guesstimated he was six foot one and maybe two years older than me. He looked pretty normal for a ruthless lawyer's kid, but he was, without question, the spitting image of his devil-spawn dad, all dark good looks and confident charisma. Instinctually, I clawed my nails into the scratchy upholstery on the arms of my chair.

Mom faltered. "Dan—"

"Sorry for coming up here." He turned, lowering his blue eyes on me. "But I didn't want Trinity to toss me out before I got to talk to her."

Mom gave him a long, considering look. Apparently, he didn't set off any warning bells because, after giving him a "you seem okay" nod, she stepped out of the doorway to let him in. Then she gave me one of her "behave yourself" glares and motioned for me to push the curtain of hair out of my face. (All the better to see you, my dear.) Mothers! Only after I dutifully flipped my hair behind my shoulders, and gave her a testy scowl, did she go downstairs to leave me alone with Devlin's progeny.

I crossed my arms over my chest, locking my mental body armor into place. Of course, my tough-as-nails demeanor probably seemed less intimidating in an itty-bitty black bikini. Mom had obviously been an easy mark, but I refused to be swayed.

He stepped into the room with hesitation, keeping a wary eye on me—probably because of the drop-dead-and-fry glower I had aimed at him.

Seeing nowhere else to sit, he lowered himself to the floor, his back against the side of my bed.

I swiveled my desk chair to face him and, taking full advantage of my elevation, peered down at him like a bug at my feet. "What do you want?"

One of his eyebrows jerked up in surprise.

"Blunt. Okay, I can do that." He braced his hands on the floor, locked his gaze with mine, and bent toward me with unflinching intensity. "My father is a power-hungry, egotistical 'slimeball' who'll do anything to win a case."

I clenched my stomach muscles as if someone had sucker punched me. Dan noticed the reflex and his eyes skimmed my bare tummy before shifting away. I kept playing it cool. "And?"

He leaned back and studied me. "Damn. You're tough."

I cocked my head and held my silence, waiting for him to fill the gap.

"And I thought you should know," he added.

"Because?"

He gritted his teeth. "Because, because I'm sick of him getting away with it. How freakin' twisted is it that he gets paid to set criminals free?"

"Your dad's an immoral scumbag," I said flatly.

"You have no idea," he agreed.

"Not a daddy's boy?"

"Far from."

"You were in court every day," I accused.

"So were you."

"What is this?" I asked, motioning to the interaction between us. "Vengeance?"

"Redemption."

His answer surprised me. "You didn't do anything."

"No, but I feel responsible," he explained.

The son repenting for his father's sins? "Why should I believe you?"

He shrugged. "You don't have to."

I didn't know what to think. Was this something his dad had put him up to? Or did he really just have some mega parental probs? I couldn't imagine anybody loathing their own father. Either way—I had one last question to ask. "Why tell me?"

"I saw you and the Delais on the news last month, when they showed the memorial service. And then, today, when the sentence was announced, it just got me thinking again. Rafe should be locked up for life, not checking into some mental motel—and it's all my dad's fault. Part of me wants to tell the Delais they're right about Rafe, but that seems like—"

"A very bad idea."

He nodded and ran a hand through his dark brown hair. "And I've been thinking about you, too. I know that loser reporter revealed your name. That had to suck."

I gave him my best droll, "Gee, ya think?" expression.

"I remember seeing you every day in the courtroom," he continued, "and, well, it seems to me, maybe the Delais aren't the only victims in all this."

I narrowed my eyes. "I'm no victim."

"No," he smartly agreed. "I know that now." He stood and shoved his fists into the front pockets of his jeans. "Anyhow, I just wanted you to know . . ." He gave a self-deprecating laugh. "I don't know what. Maybe that not everyone is like Rafe or my dad."

"Good to know," I drawled, even though I

was far from believing he was the antithesis of his father.

Dan laughed then. Really laughed. All robust and toasty. Despite myself, a wisp of a smile tickled my lips. Why did Satan's son have to be so cute?

"I like your style, Trinity."

I knew he wasn't referring to my swimsuit. Then again his eyes definitely showed some appreciation. I warmed under his hot blue gaze.

"If you ever need anything . . ."

He left the offer hanging in the air and I acknowledged it with the barest nod, my smile gone. There was no chance I'd ever ask him for anything, no matter how cute he was. How could I ever trust Robert Devlin's son?

Dan's smile slipped. "You never know," he finally said, as if in direct response to my thoughts.

Then I watched the question I'd been expecting the entire time emerge in his eyes.

"Did you really—?"

"Yeah," I interrupted. "I really dreamed about Kiri."

He nodded in acceptance. "Well, hopefully she and Rafe Stevens will stay out of your dreams from now on."

At that moment, ignorance was bliss. But Rafe had barely gotten started with me.

Chapter 3

ONE MONTH LATER

*M*acabre montage. That's the best way to describe the wicked dream I had just bolted awake from. Scratch dream—*definite* nightmare. Despite shaking my head, the choppy pictures were burned into my eyeballs whether I stared wide-eyed in the dark or squeezed them shut. No fuzzy images this time. They'd been brutally clear.

. . . Ice bath. Unmerciful and unrelenting dunkings. Gasps for air. Body shudders from the cold. Explosive chest pain. Revival.

. . . Blisters. Shaved scalp. Mustard powders rubbed on baby-soft skin. Burning. Irritation and

contagion. Sickly, puss-oozing scabs.

. . . Bloodletting. Spring-loaded lancet. Perforated veins. Red pools of humanity leaking to the floor.

. . . Poison. Ceaseless vomiting. Debilitating emptiness. Last slither of soul is purged.

. . . Shocks. Hands and feet restrained. Head lashed to the table. Electrodes affixed to the skull.

The victim's eyes. Afraid to look. Fearful of the terror there.

Eyes not wide with animalistic fear but glittery with manic acceptance.

Excitement. Euphoria. Energy.

Zap!

The last thing I heard in my dream before bolting awake was a whispered, "Trinity! I'm coming for you. . . ."

"Well, shit," I muttered and ran a shaky hand through my bedhead. "No more horror movies for me," I said, trying to make light of something I knew probably wasn't.

As I lay back down, covers pulled tightly beneath my chin, I knew I hadn't actually suffered any kind of lamebrain reaction to watching *Grindhouse* the night before. Neither was the dream some kind of wacked metaphor for a prob in my life. None of that. But the real, unfathomable shocker, the incomprehensible fact that still needled me, was that it hadn't been a lucid dream. *I* had not been there in any capacity. Weirdness. So what had I just seen? And why?

"Forgive me for saying so, hon, but you look like you've been drug through a knothole butt-backwards."

"Gee, thanks, Mom." I snorted. "You sure know how to stroke your daughter's ego."

She stroked my hair instead and gave me a "fess up" look.

"I didn't sleep so hot," I murmured before taking a sip of coffee. I sat on a barstool at the kitchen island in boxer shorts and a green-and-orange UM tee, feeling bleary-eyed and sleep deprived. How I wished I could take my caffeine intravenously.

Mom scrunched up her lips in a worried pucker. "Another nightmare?"

"Yeah," I reluctantly admitted. "No biggie. I

haven't had one for a while." I didn't want to worry her about something neither one of us had any control over.

"What was it about?"

I frowned into my coffee cup, not sure I wanted to give voice to the images in my head.

"Trin," she gently prodded.

I chugged my Go Juice and then blurted out the details of my vile vision in one breathless, caffeine-powered confession.

She gave a low whistle. "Definite nightmare, kiddo. You should stay away from horror movies."

Despite myself, I laughed. Like mother, like daughter, which in my case wasn't a bad thing. "That had nothing to do with it."

"I take it this one wasn't 'fuzzy'?"

"Not even."

"Do you think this has anything to do with my trip?" she asked. "Maybe I shouldn't go."

"No," I said firmly. "You should go. You *are* going."

"I don't know . . ." She faltered.

"I do." I laid my hand over hers. "It's time you put yourself first. This art trip to Europe, *Europe*, is your dream of a lifetime."

"Yeah, but my instructor, Doris, said the college offers this trip every two years; I could wait until the next one."

"No way." I shook my head. "This dream had nothing to do with you. I promise. Like you said, it's just a normal reaction to all the drama. I'm sorry I mentioned it. I'm driving you to the airport in two hours. End of story."

"You're sure?" she asked with a squeeze of my hand. "I won't be easy to reach."

I knew if I wanted her to stay she would. Without regrets. Without thought for herself. Suddenly overwhelmed by my love for her, and hers for me, I swallowed hard before I could answer.

"Sure."

"Has something made you think about Rafe again?" she asked with gentle concern.

"No." I shook my head. "I really haven't thought about him much since Dan's visit last month." But I *had* thought about Dan. A lot. I'd never confess it, not even under oath, but my daydreams were my own and he was the hot star. Yet, now, last night's terror was haunting me. For hours, I'd thought of nothing else and I'd only been able to conclude one thing. "This dream was just—different."

"Different how?"

"Well, like I've said before, I wasn't in it. I didn't interact with anyone. It was more like I was a disassociated observer, and even though I knew it was Rafe, he was faceless. Just shadows and silhouettes, except for the close-up of his eyes." I shuddered as I remembered his gleeful gaze. "It had to be a nightmare, Mom. A product of my imagination. Right? No one in their right mind, not even Rafe, would enjoy that kind of torture. Would they?"

"I don't know, baby." Her warm hazel eyes sparked with worry. "One person's torture is another person's pleasure."

"Gag."

"Definite gag." She held the coffee carafe

aloft and I nodded for a refill.

"Try to put it out of your mind," she suggested as she poured. "They threw that bastard's key away thirty-one days ago."

"Not that you're counting," I said with a snort, but it was a relief to know he couldn't come after me like he'd threatened to in the dream.

"Not that I'm counting," she readily agreed. "But seriously, it sounds as though you just had a normal nightmare."

I arched my eyebrows.

"Relatively speaking," she corrected. "Let's face it, you've been through enough to give anyone nightmares. And the good thing is you're having your first non-lucid dreams. Maybe there's hope for more. Normal dreams, I mean. Preferably only the pleasant ones. Could be you'll outgrow your visions."

I snorted. "They're not like Bratz dolls or braces. I don't think I'll just 'outgrow' my dreams."

"Maybe, maybe not. Adults aren't as open to psychic experiences. Our brains are hardwired to think logically, not intuitively."

"Could be, but I think I'm just naturally disturbed."

As it happened, I wasn't the only one. . . .

Chapter 4

BeckhamsBabe: It's Thursday! R u dressed for sexcess?

Night_Shade: LOL. Not yet, but I bought a BLUE dress. As ordered.

BeckhamsBabe: Yes! I want pics and full deets.

Night_Shade: It's gonna b a bore without u.

BeckhamsBabe: STFU. Make ur own fun. Go 4 the hottest guy and bat your baby blues.

My fingers hovered over the keyboard. As far as I was concerned the hottest guy I knew would be nowhere near Mariah's birthday bash.

Sheesh! Why couldn't I stop thinking about Dan Devlin?

He's the freakin' enemy's son, for heaven's

sake. Am I perverse? One of those twisted women who only fall for unattainable men? Would I be marrying a death row inmate next?

No. No. That's crazy talk.

Dan was just incredibly sweet. I mean, he'd made a point to find me and see if I was okay. Who does that? Certainly not the news vultures who'd like nothing better than to peck my carcass clean. It was simply Dan's kindness that left a lasting impression and not his gorgy good looks or pinchable, tight ass.

Okay, maybe they made a teensy, tiny impact on me.

Too bad he wasn't from a different gene pool . . . or a different lifetime.

But I couldn't help wondering—

Night_Shade: What if he's got a bad rep?

BeckhamsBabe: <VBG> All the better.

I shook my head. Typical Coral.

BeckhamsBabe: Got some1 in mind?

I couldn't tell her. Not because I didn't trust her. I did. Implicitly. But because it skeeved me out. I didn't want to tell her because of my own embarrassment. Before I could type a response Coral wrote:

BeckhamsBabe: If it's Colin Douglas STAY AWAY!!!

Night_Shade: Ew. As if. Man whore.

BeckhamsBabe: Then who?

Night_Shade: No1. Hypothetical.

BeckhamsBabe: Bad side of the streets go 4 it. Bad side of the sheets (AKA Colin), just say no.

I chuckled.

Night_Shade: No worries. Chances r I'll be in bed by 10. Ahem. Alone.

BeckhamsBabe: Don't u dare! Find a date!

"Like it's so easy," I muttered out loud. Coral had been gone a month and besides buying the blue dress, I hadn't completed *any* of my "homework." Veering the conversation, I typed:

Night_Shade: Have ur pants traveled yet?

BeckhamsBabe: Sadly, no. ☺

Night_Shade: Bummer. But, it's better that way, *Bridget*.

BeckhamsBabe: LOL. Guess so. G2G. Time 4 drills.

Night_Shade: Toodles.

54

BeckhamsBabe: TTYT. Have fun!

I x'd out of the IM with a smile on my face. Coral might be far away, but she wasn't gone. Lucky for us she got a fifteen-minute break each day for computer access. It wasn't much, but I'd take it.

Before our chat fest I'd dropped off my teary mom at the airport and then went shopping. My assigned task—find a blue dress— sounded simple enough, but without Coral's bullying, er, guidance, it had taken hours. I confess, like a devil on my shoulder, I heard her harpy admonishments in my head anytime my hand strayed to black. Finally, I settled on a low-cut dress with a handkerchief skirt. Coral would be so proud! But aside from hearing her imaginary cheers, and an admittedly killer fit that enhanced my curves, the biggest selling point of the dress was the indigo color.

The exact same shade as Dan's eyes.

Sigh.

I couldn't explain this felonious crush. It just persisted despite my distaste for his dad.

Frustrated, I stood before the full-length

mirror attached to the back of my bedroom door and held the dress in front of me.

No matter. The dress sizzled and I would work it. Who cared if it happened to be the color of his eyes? As soon as I met the hottie of the party he-who-should-not-be-thought-of would be permanently forgotten. Satisfied with my plan, but nervous that I'd be attempting to do something so bold without my wingwoman at my side, I hung the dress in my closet and let out a huge yawn.

I'd dashed home to catch Coral at four. Now it was nearly five and I was wiped out. A quick nap before the party sounded— YAWN—like the perfect pepper-upper. I kicked off my flip-flops, shirked my shorts, and crawled under the covers in my panties and a tank top. I thought about watching TV for a little while, but nixed that idea in favor of Scott Westerfeld's newest sci-fi adventure. A couple paragraphs into the book my eyes started to droop. As I drifted off I imagined dancing on the beach, under the stars, with Dan.

But I should've stuck to my daydreams because my sleep was haunted. . . .

Hours later, having slept through the party, I stood in a darkened tunnel in my dream where I could faintly hear someone calling my name. I concentrated hard, trying to pinpoint the origin. Following the sound of the voice, I came upon a television. Its glowing face offered the only light in this strange setting. Onscreen, a heavily made-up blond TV evangelist smiled at me. "Trinity," she said. Then someone invisibly rewound the frame and she repeated my name. "Trinity."

"Yes?" I asked warily and the channel switched to another program.

"I'm."

Switch.

"Coming."

Switch.

"For."

Switch.

"You, you, yooooou," a famous actress's

57

voice echoed as she plummeted off a cliff.

"No!" I screamed before bolting awake. Across from me, the black-and-white static of an offline network glowed on my TV. The TV I had never turned on. Sheer, unadulterated terror punched me into motion and I scrambled out of bed.

I hopped into my shorts and then shoved clothes into an oversized backpack with little care about whether any of the garments would actually go together or not. Fortunately, most of my don't-notice-me attire is black and thereby goes with anything. But really, how important is fashion when you're on the run?

Panties, socks, toothbrush, swimsuit, cash, cell, flashlight, pocketknife. I shoved anything and everything I could into my pack. Including the blue dress. Why? I don't know. I wasn't thinking. I was on panic-pilot. My gut instinct screamed I should bolt. Somehow, some way, Rafe Stevens had gotten out of the mental hospital and he was fixated on me, he was coming for me, he would hurt me.

I didn't just fear it—

I *knew* it.

"Getawaygetawaygetawaygetawaygetaway" played like a skipping CD in my head. The one-note survival mantra didn't allow room for logical thinking. Where was I going? How was I getting there? What was I going to do? I didn't even entertain the questions; I just packed in blind hysteria. Then I fled down the stairs and out the door with one thought in mind.

Getawaygetawaygetawaygetawaygetaway.

Chapter 5

Daniel Devlin slid into the booth across from me looking both wary and wonderful in his Abercrombie & Fitch oxford shirt and low-rise jeans. I'd tried to smooth away my rough edges before his arrival, but there was only so much a comb and concealer could do for a girl who'd had little sleep and lots of caffeine.

"You don't look too good," he said flatly.

Just what I wanted to hear from a hot guy. Grimacing, I gave my wrinkled tank top a self-conscious tug. Guess my touch-up was all for naught.

"Sorry, I just meant . . . bad dream?" he asked, the corners of his blue eyes crinkling in concern.

"You could say that."

I'd been sitting in a Denny's since three a.m. sucking down coffee and trying to alleviate the suspicious stares of the waitstaff with sugary politeness as I attempted to figure out my next step. More than a few times I'd pulled my backpack onto my lap and warred with the idea of returning home. And at least a hundred times I flipped open my cell to call my mom, but I couldn't ruin her trip. Especially when I really didn't have a handle on the sitch.

Instead I played twenty questions. Was I overreacting? Jumping at shadows? Letting my imagination get the best of me? After all, this was my first night alone. Maybe I felt more anxious about Mom being gone than I realized. In the end, I chose to follow my instincts and stay out of harm's way.

Around five-thirty a.m., and five cups of coffee later, inspiration—or maybe it was desperation—nudged me.

"If you ever need anything—."

I'd waited another hour, wondering if I was about to invite help from one demon to fight another. At the rise of the sun I capitulated and made the call. His husky voice had made me feel warm and safe, but logic dictated that I ignore desire in favor of defense.

Now, he was here to save the day. . . .

"I never thought I'd hear from you," Dan said now that he was sitting in front of me.

"I never thought I'd call you," I returned with a shrug, "but you said if I ever need anything—"

He arched an eyebrow in surprise. "Of course. What do you need?"

What do I need? Good question.

First, I had to tell this virtual stranger I'd gone on the run because of a nightmare. If he'd thought me slightly loony before he'd think me positively Daffy Duck now. And how exactly do you tell someone you need to use them?

"Uh, well, uh . . ." I stammered.

"I take it this has something to do with the Rafe Stevens case?" he prompted.

I nodded.

"Did you dream about him?"

Again I nodded and gratefully let him lead the way.

"Is someone else in danger?"

Three nods and I'm out. Gee, that wasn't so hard after all. I stifled an inappropriate giggle, realizing I might be a tad slaphappy from fatigue and bone-melting relief, but I was no longer alone.

"Who?" he asked.

Ooh, bummer, it appeared the oh-so-easy close-ended questions were *finito*. Sobriety slammed into me. Now came the sticky details or embarrassing lack thereof.

"Trinity, who's in danger?" he demanded.

"Me," I whispered.

When his mouth slammed shut and he stared at me, I wasn't sure how to interpret his reaction. So I cleared my throat, looked him straight in the eye, and repeated myself for clarity. "It's me. I'm the one in danger."

He remained mute and I squirmed in my seat. I hadn't whispered the second time so I knew he'd heard me. Why wasn't he saying anything? I hate uncomfortable chasms of silence so I started to trickle out a few pertinent details. "I kept dreaming about him . . . blah blah . . . unbelievable torture . . . blah blah and blah . . . said he's coming for me . . . blah . . . packed panties and a pocketknife . . . blah, blah . . . talked to me through the TV . . . blah . . . I ran."

Okay, maybe I GUSHED every possible deet, even the unimportant ones.

And yet, still nothing from Dan.

I sat on the backs of my hands and vowed to hold silent so he'd be forced to speak. Was he about to laugh at me and send me home? Had I made a mistake in giving him a chance? Did he plan to walk awa—

He stood.

"Hey!" When the early-bird crowd glared at my disruption I tossed them a careless smile and a wave. "Sorry, folks. Back to your regularly scheduled Grand Slams." I gripped Dan's arm. "Please," I hissed under my breath. "Don't leave. I'm not joking here."

"I know you're not," he said with steely

seriousness. "That's why we have to go."

I released my clench on his well-muscled arm so I could grab my backpack.

He tossed a twenty onto the table and, taking my hand in his, led me out of the restaurant.

Okay—I admit it—I loved the feel of his warm hand in mine, but his get-up-and-go attitude scared me a bit. "Where are we going?" I asked.

"The best place to find answers," he said.

"Smoky Hill Library?" I asked with a quizzical tilt of my head.

"No, the South Florida Mental Health Facility." He opened the passenger door on his Ford Ranger and tossed my backpack into the middle of the bench seat.

I took two steps away from the truck. "Are you crazy?" I balked. "Why don't I just stand on a street corner with a sandwich board that says, VICTIM HERE?"

"How else are we going to find out what's going on with Rafe?" he asked.

"Couldn't we just call and ask? Use your

name and connections," I carelessly suggested. To be honest, I'd already thought of going to the hospital on my own, but sometimes ignorance is bliss. Okay, maybe not bliss. But I was more afraid of what I might learn going there than I was of burying my head in the sand.

"Ah," he said, "so that's why you called me."

"I, uh, it's not—" I quickly realized what I'd just admitted. I could've lied, but if I was going to drag him into this—and I didn't exactly know what *this* was, or how dangerous it might be—he certainly had a right to know what little truth I could offer him. "I'm sorry." I placed my hands over my heart. "Truly. I just didn't know what to do. You offered your help and, yeah, I thought having Robert Devlin's son as an ally might help."

He stared at me for a moment, his face closed and expressionless, and then he gave me a hand up into his truck. "If Rafe escaped," he added, casually picking up where we'd left off, "it should be on every news channel and radio station and it's not."

That's it? He didn't plan to ditch me? "Listen,

Dan," I started slowly. "If you want to back out—"

"No." He threw the truck into reverse. "I'm with you. I don't want Rafe to hurt anyone else. There's enough blood on my family's name as it is."

"Maybe I'm wrong," I said. "Maybe it *was* just a dream."

"And maybe you're right, but there's only one way to find out for sure if Rafe has escaped."

Great, just great, I thought. Here I was trying to run *from* a killer and who was taking me toward him? Dan: the shark attorney's son . . . whom I'd just insulted.

Maybe I was the mental one.

Do you believe every building has a personality?

I do.

First, there's the facade. In my opinion, a building's "face" is usually the biggest indicator of character, but you can't sense a structure's true disposition until you walk through its front door and experience its aura.

Usually, the exterior feeling a place gives off will match its interior, but occasionally the two totally clash. South Florida Mental Health Facility, for instance, has a major schizo aura.

The place is located on one hundred acres of lush land. Built in 1876, it resembles a pristine plantation house with unblemished white paint, heavy shutters, and a wide balcony and porch with pretty scalloped trim. Green hedges, plum Blazing Stars, fragrant orange blossoms, and vibrant hibiscus flowers add to the resortlike atmosphere, but looks can be deceiving.

I didn't tune into the disharmony right away, but when I stepped through the front doors, a wave of fear ricocheted through me. I thought at first it was a gut reaction to the smell of disinfectant. Then, too, I really didn't want to be there.

"You understand the plan, right?" I whispered to Dan as we approached the information desk.

"I believe so. I *use*"—he put extra emphasis

on the word—"my name to get access to Rafe. Sound about right?"

"Yesss," I hissed through gritted teeth. "But then what?"

"Relax, Trinity. I can talk my way through anything."

"Gee, wonder who you got that little trait from."

The dirty look he gave me said my sarcasm was not appreciated.

"Wait!" I grabbed his elbow and yanked him to a stop. "Maybe we should leave. I have a bad feeling about this. Let's just go home and pretend none of this ever happened."

"Fine. If that's what you want," he offered.

I sagged in relief and pivoted on my heel.

"Just answer one question," he continued.

I closed my eyes and fisted my hands. He'd just said he could talk his way through anything and yet I still turned back to him.

"Have any of your dreams *not* come true?" He looked at me intently.

And, there it was: Score 1, Dan Devlin.

"That's what I thought," he said, raising a smug eyebrow.

He approached the information desk with a confident smile. "Hi," I heard him say. "I'm Mr. Devlin, here to see Rafe Stevens."

Chapter 6

"What do you mean he's unable to accept visitors?" Dan asked with an impressive amount of entitlement.

"Sir," the old woman with a poodle perm began, "according to our computer records he's not allowed visitation."

"I'm sure there's been some mistake," Dan insisted.

"No mistake," she volleyed back.

Switching tactics, Dan casually leaned an elbow on the counter and gave her a disarming wink. "Come on, sweetheart," he cajoled. "All you have to do is check my name and you'll see I'm on his approved contact list."

Whoo boy! The press had dubbed Dan's

dad "Debonair Devlin"—he could charm even the most hostile of witnesses—and, apparently, this apple hadn't fallen far from the tree.

"Ooh," she cooed, "you *are* on the list, Mr. Devlin. But someone has recently placed a block on his patient account. I'm so sorry."

"I understand," he responded with a patient smile. "Then just let me speak with his physician, Dr. Wrens."

The woman blanched and took a step away from the counter. "I'm afraid I can't do that."

Hmm. Something smelled hinky in the wacky ward and it wasn't the patients.

"Why not?" I asked, breaking my silence. "Is Dr. Wrens here?"

The woman wrung her hands and looked around—*everywhere* but at us. "Well, miss, he's, uh, that is, he—"

"He's dead," announced a craggy voice behind us.

In unison, Dan and I whirled around. "Dead!?!"

Another day I would've laughed at our precise comic timing, but this news wasn't funny. I fought the urge to bolt.

"Yup, dead," replied the maintenance man, who appeared as gray and nondescript as his coveralls. His name was stenciled on the breast pocket. *Milt.*

"Get back to work," the old woman hissed. Her directive sent our informant shuffling away, which prompted Dan's attention back to the desk. I, however, kept my eye on Milt, who struck me as an odd blend of affable yet creepy. As if he'd felt my gaze, Milt darted down a hallway and motioned for me to follow. I acknowledged his request with a nod before quickly turning back to the counter.

"Peg," Dan beseeched the woman, honing in on her name tag. "Is it true Dr. Wrens has died?"

"It is," she answered curtly, her curls too skull tight to sway when she bowed her head, "but that's all I can tell you. I'm sorry. You'll simply have to return some other time to see your client." She plunked a THIS DESK IS TEMPORARILY CLOSED sign down on the counter and hurried away without a backward glance.

"Correct me if I'm wrong," I said, directing a smirk at Dan, "but it seems you couldn't talk your way through her. No?"

Dan scowled.

"It's okay," I soothed, patting his shoulder. "We all meet our match at some point."

"Shut up," he growled.

I mimed zipping my lips and then grabbed his arm and tugged him toward the arch I'd seen Milt go under.

"We're not going anywhere until we get some answers," Dan said, stopping in his tracks. "Peg'll be back."

I wiggled my mouth to remind him I couldn't talk. His forehead v'd in a frown, but he reached out and unzipped my lips. I tried to hide the shiver that went through me as his fingers traced the line of my mouth. "I, uh . . ." I licked my lips to erase the tingles and walked away to hide my discomfort. "I agree we need to get answers," I said over my shoulder, making sure he'd follow, "but another round with Peg would only batter the rest of your ego." When we turned the corner Milt stood there, waiting, shoulder pressed to the wall. "Here's some answers," I told Dan.

Milt's shifty gaze darted toward us and then over our shoulders to see if anyone had followed. Seeing we were alone, he trained his focus on me.

"I know you."

"Yeah?"

"You're Dream Girl."

I winced at the superhero moniker.

Dan stepped in front me. "She hasn't dreamed about *you*," he said coolly.

Ah, perhaps chivalry wasn't dead. There's nothing like a guy willing to guard you with his own body. But, despite Dan's gallant gesture, I stepped around him. "What do you know about Dr. Wrens?" I asked Milt.

The maintenance man's upper lip danced with the quiver of a nervous tic.

Ooh-kay, maybe this guy was crazier than creepy. Perhaps it was time to fly outta this cuckoo's nest. I started to take a retreating step when Milt said, "Tell me something."

"Yesss," I hissed in exasperation with an

impatient eye roll. "I really *did* dream about Kiri. Sheesh, what's the big —?"

"I'm not talking about that," he interrupted. "I know you tried to save her," he said. By the look of appreciation on his face, you'd have thought Milt was my biggest fan. Then he pointed an accusing finger at Dan. "But his daddy let him get away with murder. Why are you together?"

Suh-nap! We had a sharp one here. Never underestimate a spooky janitor.

"Actually, Milt," I said conspiratorially, "we're teaming up to keep Rafe from hurting anyone else."

Milt rolled his lips into a tight slash before answering. "What makes you think he'd hurt another person?"

That was the million-dollar question, wasn't it? Milt and I seemed to be on the same page, so I decided to trust him with the truth.

"Because I dreamed he escaped and was coming after me."

He stood silent for a moment and then bobbed his head. "You're right," he said.

"What?" I gasped.

"Afraid so," he confirmed.

Dan wrapped an arm around my shoulder. "It's okay, Trin. We'll find him."

Before I could ask how, Milt continued. "You need to be worried about him finding *you*," he said. "Let me show you something." He pulled two laminated visitor badges out of his pocket. "Clip 'em on. As long as you wear those and stay with me there won't be trouble."

"Milt, don't take this the wrong way"—I held up my hands in a gesture of appeasement—"but how do we know you won't take us straight to him? I know you said he's gone, but—"

Milt cut me off in mid-accusation. "Guess you don't," he said. "All I can tell you is I'm trying to help."

"Why?" Dan asked, his voice gruff with suspicion.

"That'll be easier to explain when I show you what happened to him."

"What happened to him?" I repeated.

"Let me show you," Milt snapped, clearly

frustrated. But when he saw my eyes widen in response, he smoothed his nicotine-yellowed fingers over his gray hair as if to calm himself. "You won't believe me, otherwise," he said evenly.

Uncertainty and curiosity warred within me. I looked to Dan, who cupped his chin, obviously calculating risk against gain.

"We don't have any better leads," he said finally.

I sighed. "I was afraid you'd say that." *Curiosity wins; let's hope it doesn't kill this kitty.* Reluctantly, I clipped on my tag and motioned to Milt to lead the way. We trailed after him until he reached a far-removed door marked CENTRAL BASEMENT—STAFF ONLY. Milt keyed a code into the high-tech panel affixed to the right of the door. Inside the stairwell he retrieved a battery-powered Coleman lantern from a small wall-mounted shelf, then handed us two flashlights. "Backup," he explained. "You don't want to be down there in the dark."

Dark? Dark? No one said anything about a dark basement! I don't do dark basements.

"I think I saw an episode of *Supernatural*

78

like this," I whispered too loudly. "It ended badly for everyone except Dean and Sam."

Milt ignored my comment and started down the blackened stairs.

Dan and I exchanged anxious looks, but, really, what choice did we have?

"I'll be Dean," he said.

"No way," I argued. "I'm prettier."

"Fine," he capitulated. "I can do smart and sullen."

I blurted a strained giggle and closely followed him down the stairs. Mildew and rot assaulted my nose, instantly sobering me. My stomach lodged in my throat, and I shocked myself by tucking my hand into Dan's. He wrapped his fingers tight around mine and I felt comforted, if still scared. At the end of the well we came to an area that resembled half a wagon wheel laid flat. We stood at the center and tunnels shot off in different directions from its base-like spokes.

"Where are you taking us?" Dan asked in a hushed voice.

I heard the wariness in his tone and felt an

answering worry in my stomach. This was insanity. We were following a stranger to God knows where. Anything could happen to us and no one would know where we were. My fight-or-flight instincts threatened to erupt in an ugly, full-freakout kinda way when Milt finally started to give some answers.

"Used to be there were tunnels all over, but most have collapsed or been boarded. No one comes down here anymore. No one but Dr. Wrens."

"And he came down here, why?" I asked, shivering from the cooler temperature and the palpable malice surrounding us.

Milt turned to me, his face looking shadowy and skeletal in the glow of our lights. I shivered harder.

"You know anything about asylums?" he began.

"Like what?" I asked, not sure what he meant.

"How they was way back when."

I looked at Dan and he shook his head.

"I only know a little," I offered, "from stuff

I've read. I know patients used to be tortured."

Milt grunted. "You know enough, then," he said before heading down a dank tunnel to the right. The walls were tinged green with wet slime and it smelled like a cavern. "Dr. Wrens, he, um, was a fan of old techniques."

"Wait a minute." I let go of Dan's hand and grabbed Milt by the arm. "Do you mean he tortured patients?"

Milt stared at my hand and didn't answer. Didn't move. Didn't breathe.

"Sorry," I mumbled and let go.

He reverently placed his hand over the spot my palm had touched, then went on to explain, "Doc preferred to call them 'therapies,' but yeah. He did experiments on one patient in particular."

"Rafe?" Fear and nausea collided inside me. It was one thing to hope he'd be locked up for the rest of his life, even to imagine kismet kicking his ass, but I could never take pleasure in anyone, even Rafe, being tormented at the hands of another.

"Yup, Rafe," Milt confirmed. He stopped

before a chain-locked double door. "Doc liked to experiment on him because he didn't break."

I shuddered as I watched Milt remove an antique key from his coverall pocket. He unlocked a rusty padlock and pulled the heavy chain through the steel. Suddenly, flashes of my nightmare assaulted me. Even without seeing, I *knew* what hid behind the doors Milt had just swung open.

I didn't want to go in there.

Milt stepped across the threshold and lit several lanterns around the room's perimeter. Dan followed, but I didn't budge. "Trinity?"

I opened my mouth to speak. Words wouldn't come.

"It's okay," Dan assured as he took my hand and gently drew me into the room. My fingers trembled in his grasp.

"What is this place?" Dan asked Milt.

"A chamber of horrors," I whispered, suddenly fully understanding what I'd witnessed in my dreams. Releasing Dan's hand, I picked up a leather harness that lay on a steel medical cart. "This is a head restraint for shock therapy.

And that"—I pointed to, but didn't touch, an aged tin—"is mustard powder. It blisters the skin. There's also a poison here that induces brutal vomiting." I looked across the room to a freestanding tub and remembered seeing horrific ice-bath dunkings. "He nearly had a heart attack from being drowned in here, but Wrens revived him." I whirled around the room, searching it with manic intensity. "And somewhere, there's some kind of gadget that pokes you until you bleed. He was poked over and over, and ov—"

"It's called a lancet," Milt interrupted. A look of utter confoundment creased his face. "How did you know?"

"This is what you saw in your nightmare," Dan insisted. "Isn't it?"

"I, I thought it was just a bad dream," I stammered. "But it was Rafe. I saw what was done to him. I was in his head!"

"In his head?" Milt asked.

"I saw everything through his eyes. I don't know how I did it. It's never happened before, but you were right. He didn't break." I groaned in disgust as I remembered the feelings that had coursed through me—fear, then omnipotence. "Rafe liked it. It made him feel powerful."

"Didn't just *feel* that way," Milt corrected me. "He *was* that way."

"What do you mean?" I asked.

"Something happened when Doc hooked him to the machine." Milt placed a jittery hand on the evil equipment he spoke of. "He used to leave him on the table for hours, until Rafe fell asleep, then when he was off guard, dreaming, the doc would zap him."

"How cruel," I cried, imagining myself on the table.

"First Rafe fought hard to stay awake, but then he'd get on the table and conk out sooner and sooner, almost like he wanted to get juiced." Milt shook his head at the memory. "Then, yesterday, he fell asleep before he even got hooked up. I couldn't believe it when Doc turned the dials and Rafe didn't budge. Then Doc cranked it higher and I swear Rafe smiled in his sleep. Doc kept turning and turning." Unconsciously, Milt fingered the dial back and forth. "Then, finally, Rafe's eyes popped open and he started hollering, but not like he was hurting, more like he was, um, charging up."

"You're not serious," Dan said in an incredulous tone.

"No, no, really," Milt insisted. "It was like he was getting amped up. The whole thing scared the bejesus outta me. I went to yank the plug, but the machine blew up." He pointed to a blackened area on the box. "I figured his brains had to be fried, but he unstrapped himself, sat up, and—I swear to the Almighty—said, 'Thanks, Doc.'"

"No freakin' way," Dan scoffed.

I could tell Dan was ready to ditch Milt, but something told me to stay and hear him out. I turned to our humble informant. "That kind of shock should've killed Rafe," I protested.

"Should've," he agreed, "but I think his brain just stretched instead of snapped."

"I don't understand," I said as goose bumps caterpillared their way up my arms.

"About three weeks after Doc started doing this he told me he dreamed about Rafe," Milt explained. "I figured it was guilt talking, but he kept having dreams and they got more 'n' more real. It got so bad he was afraid to sleep by himself at home, so he'd crash in his office. That didn't help," he continued. "In one dream Rafe grabbed his arm and when the doc yanked it away he got scratched. He woke up with a scratch on his arm in the exact same spot."

"Coincidence," Dan refuted. "It was probably there before he went to sleep."

Milt nodded. "That's what Doc said. Then I had a dream."

"And?" I asked.

"I could have sworn Rafe was right there. He seemed as real as you."

"Did he touch you? Hurt you?" Dan asked.

"No, but—"

"See," Dan exclaimed with assurance, "just coincidence. It's messed up to think getting zapped made him able to enter people's dreams. Besides, Trinity doesn't go into other people's dreams, they come to her." He aimed a look of disgust at Milt. "I'm thinking the two of you did enough down here to give anyone nightmares."

"Dan!" I scolded, feeling strangely protective of Milt.

"What?" Dan asked, incredulous. "Seems to me Milt here played Igor to Dr. Frankenstein. That would make him an accomplice."

"I didn't have a choice," Milt said. "The doc threatened me. Said I could help or get hooked up." His entire body visibly shuddered. "He did that to me once," he whispered, a haunted expression on his face. "I, I couldn't take it again." His eyes pleaded for my understanding.

"I know. It's okay," I told him gently. "This is all on Dr. Wrens."

"Why didn't you do something to stop it?" Dan insisted.

"He'd have killed me," Milt cried.

"You should have—"

"Stop!" I yelled at Dan. "This isn't a courtroom. Quit interrogating him."

Dan took a step back as if I'd slapped him. Maybe it was my implication that he was acting like his father. "Fine," he said. "At least Dr. Wrens got what was coming to him."

"That's because Rafe murdered him," Milt

said. "Through his dreams."

"That's impossible," I said, unconvinced. "Dreams are just confessions of the mind, there's no physicality involved. I could see why you might think that, but—"

"Are you high?" Dan hollered, interrupting me. "This is insanity." He paced the room. "Of course it is. We are, after all, in a mental hospital."

I ignored him and turned back to Milt. "What did the coroner say?" I asked him.

"Heart attack," he murmured.

"There you go," Dan said, inserting himself between us. "Nothing weird about that. Karma just bit him in the ass. Maybe there's hope yet for my father."

"Dan, shut up!" I said. "This isn't about you."

This time Dan ignored *me* and turned to Milt. "Tell me why you think he's coming after Trinity," he asked pointedly.

Milt shrugged. "He blames her for being caught," he explained, "and now they share something in common."

"Dreams," I said, understanding, in a terrible instant, the whole picture.

"That's *loco*, man," Dan said.

"Is it?" I asked. "It was my dream that led the police to him. He was arrested and then tortured. Of course he blames me. And, who knows, maybe he really can dream walk in some way."

Dan looked unconvinced.

"Doesn't matter, though," I continued. "I'm used to dream visitations. Him finding me in real life, before we find him . . . that's my worry."

Dan's stony expression softened. "Mine, too, but I'll keep you safe."

My heart fluttered. How could this guy be so atrociously overbearing one moment and then so selflessly heroic the next?

"Come on. Let's get out of this dungeon," Dan said as he took hold of my elbow.

"Wait." I turned to Milt. "Thank you."

For a moment he stopped turning off lanterns and gave me a soul-searching stare. "Be careful," he warned me. "Protect your mind. Doc used to say something about dreams being windows."

"Sure." I nodded and recited something I'd heard my mom say often enough. "Dreams are windows to the soul."

"That's it." Milt's pupils dilated in fear. "But what if they're not? What if they're really doorways to the mind? And Rafe's got the key?"

Chapter 7

Some people say marriage is the one war in which you sleep with the enemy. Sadly, for me, it didn't even require a ring. Here I was at a skanky SoBe hotel on Collins Avenue ready to climb into bed with the opposing council (his son, anyhow). Not only were we *not* married, we were not even remotely attracted to each other. (Okay, that was so totally a lie.) And we couldn't seem to agree on anything. (That part was true, unless you counted catching Rafe.)

How did I get so desperate?

Dead. End.

After leaving the hospital, Dan and I headed to Dr. Wrens's bachelor pad. It made sense that Rafe might go there, knowing the place was empty. Conversation on the way over was beyond scintillating.

Dan: When we get there, I'll look around. If he's there we'll call the cops.

Me: (under my breath) Doorways to the mind?

Dan: You're not listening to that freakin' nutbar, are you?

Me: Hey! Milt isn't crazy, just a little off-kilter. You'd do well to be as open-minded as he is.

Dan: I'm open-minded, just able to filter fact from fiction. That's why I'm out here and he's in there.

Me: You're a real jerk, you know that? How is it you believe my dreams, but you're unwilling to believe him?

Dan: I'm a jerk?

Me: Just answer the question.

Long, unbearable silence, then . . .

Dan: You've proven your dreams are real. First with Kiri and now with Rafe's escape.

Aha! So he hadn't been a true believer. Not until I'd passed test number two.

Me: You know, not everything is black and white.

Dan: Sure it is. Night and day, good and evil, harmony and chaos, Spider-Man and Sandman. Everything falls on one side or the other. There's no in between.

I bit my tongue. Literally. I tasted blood.

Dan: You really think I'm a jerk?

I gave a dramatic, breathy sigh.

Me: That remains to be seen. At the moment, you're kinda . . . gray.

So, here we were now, attempting to settle down in a no-tell motel Dan had paid cash for. Making it seem even more skizzy, he had registered us as Susan and Reed Richards. That's right, geekoid "disguised" us as the Invisible Woman and her super-stretchy S.O. The fanboy at check-in had not been fooled. "Fantastic Four. *Marvel-ooous*," he drawled with a knowing wink as he handed us our key.

Standing side by side in the doorway of our room, staring at ONE double bed, nearly made me pass out. Coral would pee her pants when I told her.

Sweaty and apprehensive, I stepped in and chucked my backpack into the corner, not daring to look at Dan.

"So, um," he mumbled as he followed me in and kicked the door shut with his heel, "which side do you want?"

My head jerked up. "Siiide?" I squeaked. Clearing my throat, I tried again. "Side?"

He smiled, looking a bit bemused. "Of the bed."

I glanced nervously from the bed to him and back.

"I'll take the left."

He nodded and immediately leaped onto the right side, legs outstretched, arms tucked behind his head. He kicked off his shoes and closed his eyes.

I froze in the corner.

"I'm hungry," he murmured, without looking at me. "Are you?"

Hungry? How could he think of food right now? We were in a hotel room. Alone. Together.

I wasn't thinking about food.

He opened his eyes. "Trin?"

"Hmm." Then I snapped out of my deep freeze. "Uh, sure. I could eat."

"Great!" He bounced over to my side of the bed and rooted through the nightstand drawer for a phone book. "You like Chinese?"

I gave myself a mental slap. If he was going to act like this was no big deal so would I. I'd pretend it was a sleepover like me and Coral always had, only I doubted Dan would let me paint his nails.

"Sesame chicken, please."

"You like spicy, eh?"

"The hotter the better," I said, then flushed.

When the food arrived twenty minutes later, I admit I was famished. Fortunately, Dan had ordered enough food for a family of six. Or so I thought.

There was only one chair in the room so we pulled the small table to the end of the bed and ate side by side. At first I was acutely aware of how close we were, but then—when Dan started steam-shoveling food into his mouth—I laughed and relaxed into the moment.

"Wha'r oo 'aughing at?" he asked around a mouthful of beef and broccoli.

"You," I said with a giggle. "How can you eat like that?"

He chugged some water. "Like what?" he asked.

"Like your stomach is a black hole."

"Oh, that," he said with a grin. "Easy, my stomach *is* a black hole." He gave me a suspicious look. "You're not one of those girls, are you?"

I lifted my eyebrows. "Those girls?"

"You know, those eat-four-peas-and-you're-sooo-stuffed girls."

I snickered. "Hardly. I like food, and I have a fast metabolism."

He slurped up some lo mein noodles. "Good. I hate grazers." He handed me his carton. "Try some."

I twined my fork around some noodles and took a bite. My eyes widened in pleasure. "Yummm."

Dan gave me a "that's what I thought" nod.

Just then my phone played a few chords

from Iggy Pop's "Real Wild Child."

"Coral!" I leaped from the bed, nearly toppling the table, and scrambled around in my bag for my cell. Plunking down in the chair, I read her text.

Coral: U forgot our 4:00.

Me: Sorry! Crazy day.

Coral: Too much partying?

Me: No. Something came up.

Coral: You didn't go?!?

I winced and typed no.

Coral: Better be a good reason.

A killer coming after me seemed like a good reason, but I couldn't tell her that, so I told her something I knew would make her happy.

Me: Cute guy.

Coral: For realz?

Me: Swear.

Coral: Tell!!!

Me: Can't. He's here.

Coral: OMG! I'm dying. Tell me something.

I looked over at Dan.

Me: Dark and dreamy.

Coral: Older?

Me: 20

Coral: Woot! Go, Trin, go, Trin, go, Trin.

I grinned and then ducked my head so Dan wouldn't see.

Me: G2G. TTYL. Promise!

Coral: Better! 'Bye. XXOO.

I flipped the phone closed and shoved it back into my bag.

"Sorry," I said, sitting back next to him.

"No prob," he said around an egg roll. "Coral your friend?"

"Best."

"Were you talking about me?" he asked with a cocky smile.

I flipped my hair over my shoulder. "Hardly," I hotly denied. "She was telling me about soccer camp."

"You sure?" he asked and bumped his shoulder against mine.

"Quite!"

"So, why didn't you go with her?" he asked as he twirled a pair of unused wooden chopsticks.

"To camp?"

98

He nodded as he dug back into the lo mein.

"Not my thing." I shrugged. "She's Soccer Star, I'm Goth Girl."

He pointed his fork at me. "What's that? Like an official title? You got a sash and everything?"

I laughed. "Sash? As in, royalty?"

"Sure. Why not?"

"First, I'm not even on the radar at school and, second, if they did crown me anything it would probably be Queen of the Damned."

"Wow." He wiped his mouth with a napkin and leaned his hands back on the bed. "Negative much?"

"Um"—I gave him a "duh" eye roll—"I'm being stalked by a killer. That warrants some negativity."

"Sure, if you want to be like that," he said all flippantly. "But that wasn't always the case, right?"

I tugged at the ends of my hair. "True, but I like staying under the radar."

He studied me for a moment. "Because of your dreams?"

My gaze darted to his and my heart hammered. "Yeah," I said softly. "It makes it easier. I learn too many bad things about people."

"I get it. Staying separate gives you an emotional barrier, but it keeps you from getting close to people. That's got to be rough."

Tears burned the back of my throat. He *understood*?

"What about Coral?" he asked.

I grinned. "Coral never gave me a choice about being her friend. And she doesn't have any skeletons in her closet I might accidentally unbury."

"Does she know?"

I shook my head. "Only that I dreamed about Kiri. I let her believe it was a one-time fluke." I nibbled on the crunchy shell of an egg roll before deciding I didn't feel hungry anymore.

He arched an eyebrow. "How come you haven't told her?"

I winced. "Because I don't want her to look at me differently. She already suspects I'm hiding something."

"And yet she sticks around." He stood and started clearing the table. "Seems like you aren't protecting yourself so much as underestimating your best friend."

"You sound like my mom," I said in exasperation.

"She's a smart lady. You'll have to get past your intimacy issues eventually if you want a real relationship."

"Who are you? Dr. Phil?" I pushed the table back against the wall. "It's easy for you to dish out advice, but what if it did change things between me and Coral? Or the future Mr. Michaels?"

Dan pitched the cartons into the trash and turned to face me. "And what if it didn't? What if you had someone who understood who you really are and accepted you that way?"

I shook my head. "Who could do that?"

He laughed. "Me."

Stunned, I could only stare. "I—I—I'm going to take a shower," I stammered and then bolted for the bathroom.

As I shampooed my hair I realized for the

first time that someone, other than my mom, knew my secret and didn't look at me like I was a two-headed snake. It felt amazing. Liberating. Maybe, just maybe, Dan was right about Coral. After running confession scenarios over and over in my mind, I turned off the water and wrapped myself in the hotel's too small, too scratchy, bleach-white towel. Then I took an inordinate amount of time lotioning, combing out my hair, and brushing my teeth. I was totally stalling. But it was one thing to spend the day with Dan in the truck and quite another in the same bed.

Unfortunately, having used all the hot water and feeling wrinkly, squeaky clean, I had to come out of my hiding place. Walking out of the bathroom in boxers and a tank top, I found Dan sitting on top of the covers, scrawling notes on a hotel notepad. He looked positively scrumpdillyicious. Bare chest, bare feet, and snug jeans. Total casual sexy. My mouth watered and I briefly considered sleeping in the safety of the bathtub.

I walked to my side of the bed and lifted the

sheets. First I checked for Dan's reaction, none, then I checked for bedbugs, none. My stomach twitchy with anxiety, I climbed in and tried not to think too much about Dan's proximity. This wasn't exactly a "been there, done that" kind of sitch for me. I hadn't slept with a guy in a hotel or otherwise. And while I knew *sleeping* in this instance meant just that, it wasn't every day I crawled under the covers with a hottie.

"What're . . ." Strain tightened my vocal cords and I squeaked a bit. Clearing my throat, I tried again. "What're you doing?" I asked, my back pressed to the headboard.

Slowly, he lifted his gaze from his notes; a deep furrow at the bridge of his nose showed the depth of his concentration. When he finally looked at me the crease melted away. His gaze trailed down my wet hair to my damp tank top. I flushed and pulled the sheet on my lap higher up over my chest.

"You smell good," he murmured.

"Um, thanks." I pointed to the paper on his lap and willed my pulse to stop doing the polka.

"Working on something?"

He shook his head, as if to clear it, and gave me one more admiring glance before snapping a back-to-business look onto his face. "I made a few calls while you were in the shower."

I raised my eyebrows.

"First, I called the press and left an anonymous tip about Rafe's disappearance."

"All hands on deck."

"Exactly." He tapped his pen on the pad. "The more people looking for him, the better chance we have of finding him before he finds you."

"Did you mention the, uh—"

"Basement? Yeah, I did."

"What about Milt?"

"I kept him out of it."

"Thank you."

He shifted a bit, as if uncomfortable. "Does that win me back some points?"

Despite myself, I smiled. "Mos def." I didn't know why he cared, but I liked the fact that he did.

"Yeah, well," Dan said with a wry grin, "I

still don't believe his crazy theory."

"Ha!" I gave his shoulder a playful shove. "If dreams were doorways to the mind, I'd be *so* screwed."

Dan laughed and I basked in the moment. Here, now, I didn't see a scary resemblance to his dad. I saw a good-looking, sensitive guy who looked past the yellow caution tape blocking off my heart.

"I just wish we'd found something at Wrens's place," he said.

Yeah, that part of our day had not gone as expected.

When we first got to the doc's house Dan had slunk around the perimeter looking for Rafe. The place appeared empty, so we let ourselves in, thanks to my impressive lock-picking skills. (Don't ask.) An unmade bed, a cereal bowl and coffee cup in the sink, and a newspaper folded to the sports section on the dining table left clues to the doc's morning routine but little else. The place was surprisingly immaculate for a bachelor pad and clearly hadn't been raided by an escaped convict.

So, where had Rafe gone?

"Are you brainstorming other leads?" I asked Dan, rolling to my side to better face him on the bed.

"Yeah, I called a . . . friend and he suggested we check Rafe's home address."

Dan's hesitation over the word *friend* did not escape my notice and it gave me a bad vibe. "I see. And who is this *friend*?"

"Just a, um, lawyer," he mumbled.

He studied the pen in his hand intently, avoiding eye contact with me.

Red flags sprang up all over my mind. What was he hiding? "This friend isn't your dad, is he?"

His head snapped up. "No!"

My face must've been pinched with suspicion because he kicked in with some smooth talking.

"No worries, Trinity. I wouldn't draw my dad into this. I swear. The guy I called is just experienced with this kind of case, and I thought he might have some ideas."

I felt both appeased and apprehensive. I didn't have to worry about Daddy Dearest, but I still suspected Dan was covering up something. I plucked tiny balls of cotton fluff from the worn blanket. "What else did your friend have to say?"

"That a lot of escaped criminals head straight for home or a girlfriend's house," Dan offered. "Makes them easy to catch."

I shook my head in immediate denial. "Rafe's not your average criminal."

"No," he agreed, "but it's a place to start."

"What else?"

"Nothing really," he hedged.

"Nothing really?" I echoed, knowing he meant *something really*.

He shifted on the bed to face off with me. "I was just wondering, if you could, you know . . ."

I looked at him blankly. "Uh, no. I don't know."

"Dream about it."

I didn't know whether to be pissed or laugh in his face. I finally decided to rely on that great self-preservation standby . . . sarcasm. "And what, pray tell, would you like me to dream about?"

He must've heard the acid in my tone because he shifted—squirmed might be more accurate—and waved off his words. "Never mind."

"No, no," I insisted. "Spill it."

He frowned. "I just thought maybe you'd be able to use your . . ."

. . . If he said *powers* I'd scream bloody murder.

"Ability to find Rafe."

"How?" I asked tightly.

"I don't know, just . . ."

. . . If he said *concentrate* I'd have to hit him.

"Focus your energy on him."

"Then what'll happen?"

"Maybe you'll get a . . ."

. . . If he said *vision* I'd lock him in *the* basement.

"A vibe."

"Vibe?" I smirked.

"An intuitive feeling," he said, as if I needed

an explanation. "Then we can follow your hunch."

"Uh-huh." I drew in a deep, slow, measured breath. It didn't help. Next, I counted to ten. Then I bumped it to twenty. Mmm-kay, getting a little better. Then I hummed the word *zen* in my head, giving the (*n*) some meditative vibrato. Okay, that was even better. I felt slightly less murderous. I could do this, I could keep my cool. *Zennnnn.* Ah, centered. I locked my eyes with Dan's, then bit off each word individually like a particularly tough piece of jerky. "I. Am. Not. A. FREAKIN' SIDESHOW ACT!" I hollered the rest.

Sigh. So much for being chill.

Dan clenched his jaw but otherwise didn't react to my blast.

"I just thought—" he began, looking more irritated then apologetic.

"I know what you thought," I said. "Don't you think I haven't tried that before? My mom tested me for all kinds of things when I was a kid. 'Concentrate, Trin. What card am I holding? You can do it, Trin. Where'd I hide the remote?'" I threw my hands up in exasperation. "You know what we found out? I am *not* psychic. Patricia Arquette is more psychic than I am. People just come talk to me in my dreams. I don't want them to, but they do anyhow. I learn what they tell me, but I never have"—I made air quotes with my fingers—"'visions.' You won't see me getting that deer-in-the-headlights look Raven did on that old Disney show. Mine is just a useless *ability*, as you called it, that curses my frickin' life."

"It's not useless," Dan denied. "If it weren't for you, Rafe wouldn't have gotten caught."

"A lot of good that did," I said bitterly. I flipped back the covers and got out of bed, too wrecked to relax. "I didn't save Kiri and now he's after me." I pointed to him. "And I dragged *you* into this whole mess, so now we're both on the run."

He shook his head. "You didn't drag me into this."

I gave him a "yeah, right" look.

"It's true. I chose to help you."

"Why?"

"Because I don't want anyone else to die at Rafe's hands."

"And?" I pushed. "I know there's more to it."

My bluntness startled him. I thought at first he'd skirt the subject, but he answered with carefully weighted words. "And . . . I already told you I feel inherently responsible for my dad letting a murderer go, but if Rafe kills again then my dad may as well have handed him the weapon."

Whoa. Accomplice to murder. I thought about that for a minute. That would leave a helluva scar on Dan's psyche. And, sadly, he seemed injured enough by his father's past actions. "Do you really detest him?"

"With every damned bone in my body," he said fiercely.

"Why?" I persisted. "Isn't he just doing his job?"

Now it was Dan who barked out a bitter laugh. "He does his job, all right. At the cost of everything else."

"Okay, I get that you can't stand him and

what he represents. He's certainly not a fave of mine, either, but tell me how catching Rafe will help. What will change?" I asked. I had this niggling feeling I was missing something. . . .

Dan's gaze jumped to mine and then away. "I don't know. When Rafe's caught he'll go to jail this time. There's no amount of coaching my dad could do to stop that."

I paced a small circle across the faded carpet, trying to find the missing link in his logic. "So, you're in this to see that your dad's actions get undone?"

His eyes brightened as if I'd very helpfully put the right words into his mouth.

"Yeah . . . yeah, that's one way to put it."

Huh-uh, I didn't buy it. There was more here; I sensed it. An ulterior motive I couldn't figure out yet. But was Dan lying to me? What if he were really here on behalf of his father? What if I was part of a CYA ploy?

I narrowed my eyes. "Did you call your dad and tell him about Rafe's escape?"

"No," he said firmly. "I told you, I'm not

involving him. He'll learn it soon enough on the news."

Instinct told me he spoke the truth, but something still felt hinky. I wouldn't, couldn't, completely put my trust in Dan.

I pulled the hard-backed chair away from the small table. Straddling the seat, I laid my hands and chin on the top rung. "You think your dad'll freak?"

"Oh, yeah," Dan said. "But he'll probably call in some favors and get even more people looking for Rafe."

"That's something, I guess."

Dan stretched himself stomach down on the bed, corner to corner. Propping himself up on his forearms, he looked at me curiously. "Can I ask you something?" He held up his hand. "And I'm not trying to start a fight."

I nodded, knowing I could always refuse to answer.

"Did you ever think maybe you're limiting your powers by shunning them?"

Not that again. "Look"—I sighed in exasperation—"I want to find Rafe, too, but—"

"I'm not talking about clueing into him. I'm just saying, in general, it seems to me you really detest your ability—"

"Like you really detest your dad."

"Maybe if you learned to embrace it—"

"Like you should learn to embrace your dad?"

His jaw slammed shut audibly and he rolled to his back, staring at the ceiling. "Geesh, Trin. Let up."

Chalk up a winning mark for me. But who was the jerk now?

"Listen," I offered in a conciliatory tone, "even if I 'embraced' my ability I wouldn't develop other skills."

"Maybe," he told the acoustic tiles above. "Maybe not." He tilted his head back to look at me. "But if you accepted it you wouldn't feel so—"

"Bitter."

"I was going to say intruded upon."

Intruded upon? Was that how I felt? I pondered that outside observation for a sec. Yeah, actually it was. Every night when I dreamed and someone showed up it felt like they'd burst through my bedroom door without knocking.

"What I need is a Keep Out sign. Visitors not welcome. No solicitations. Trespassers will be prosecuted."

Dan chuckled. "I'm not sure about signage, but maybe accepting your gift will give you some power over it."

"Maybe," I said with some skepticism. "But you know what Peter Parker said—"

"With great power comes great responsibility."

I settled back on the bed and looked into Dan's eyes. "What if I can't handle it?"

He gave me a knowing smile. "Don't you get it? You already are."

Chapter 8

You already are....

Dan actually believed I handled the responsibility that came with my dreams. If he only knew how many times I'd turned my back, denied what I knew, what I *was*. How many times I'd done nothing.

How could he think me responsible?

Because you did what you could for Kiri, a voice whispered in my head. *And you're still fighting to catch Rafe.*

I lay stiffly on my back watching the orange glow of the neon motel sign penetrate the thin curtains every ten—one-thousand count. On. Off. On. Off. If only I could turn off my mind.

Dan's soft snores were comforting. Still, I

couldn't believe I was about to sleep next to a guy in a hotel that advertised "reasonable hourly rates." (Well, he slept while I practiced supine self-analysis.) Despite the lumpy mattress, Dan had fallen asleep quickly, on his side with his back to me. I guess I was the only one suffering from sexual tension insomnia. When his breathing first evened out, I placed a two-pillow barrier between us. Totally 1950s, I know, but it would at least stop him from rolling over and sprawling on top of me (not that I'd find that totally intolerable).

You don't even trust him, I chastised myself. *You're not even sure you like him. But he sure gives you tingles, and it ain't your Spidey sense going off.*

Apparently, lust is indiscriminate.

I rolled to my side and spooned with the pillow barrier. The irritating voice in my head finally quieted and I let myself relax a bit. It wasn't like Dan was going to cop a feel in the middle of the night or jump me. He'd managed to fall asleep without a single concern for our intimate situation. So I decided I was grown-up enough to do the same.

Comfortable in my newfound sophistication I snuggled deep into the covers and slowly let myself drift to sleep with this very mature thought in my head: *My mom would so totally freak!*

Have you ever seen a holographic image on TV or in the movies? You know how they're transparent and kinda flicker and fade?

That's how Rafe showed up in my dream that night.

I can't say I was entirely surprised to see him. I figured he'd stop by for a visit sooner or later. As far as I could tell, he wasn't any different from the other cast of characters that habitually dropped by unannounced. Generally speaking, the interlopers in my dreams don't have any special abilities. They don't purposefully project themselves into my world. It's more like they're crying out in their sleep and, because my ability is set to "receive," I tune in to them. Lucky me.

Knowing what I did about Rafe, I figured his visit was more planned than providence.

Still, this was just a phantasm of his soul. Amorphous. Safe. In fact, he looked even more tenuous than my nocturnal company usually did. Almost ghostly, in fact.

In my dreamscape, we stood outside the gates of the mental hospital. The deep shadows of night made the building look even more malignant. It made sense that Rafe would pick a place we were both familiar with.

As far as villains go, he looked pretty innocuous, just your average white middle-aged male with a receding hairline. He could have been your broker or an insurance salesman. Yet, if you looked closely at his brown eyes, deep-set under heavy brows, a disturbing darkness lurked there.

Standing across from me, he looked battered and worn. Remembering what Wrens had put him through, I felt momentarily sorry for him, but any sympathy I had quickly dissolved when he stepped forward and tried to grab me. Never, *ever*, had one of my visitors attempted to touch me. It was bad enough that they barged into my psyche, but trying to make physical contact was an egregious violation of my personal space!

In self-defense, I backed away and held up my arms. He swiped wildly at me, but since he had no physical mass his hands just made shimmering arcs through the air.

"Knock it off!" I hollered.

My command shocked him and he jerked to a stop.

"What do you want?" I demanded.

He pointed to me and I watched him mouth the word *you*, but his projection was muted. His inability to speak enraged him. He squeezed his throat and his face flushed purple. For a moment his presence came in clearer. Then I heard him repeat "you" in a stuttery voice.

"Oooh, big surprise," I snarked. "Well, you can't have me. Go back where you came from."

His lips lifted in a cruel smile and I heard him whisper, "Good idea." Then he dug his fingernails as hard as he could into his other arm.

Suddenly, his image sharpened and I gasped in shock. He looked three-dimensional!

When he stopped his self-mutilation I saw little bloody crescent shapes mar his arm where he'd broken the skin.

I stumbled back in shock and heard him snicker in response.

"Still feeling brave?" he asked, loud and clear.

Ohmygod. What was happening here?

He seemed to relish the fresh waves of pain he got when he flexed his arm, as if the pain were giving him power. How could that be?

Nervously, I watched as the angry red welts on his arm lightened. As they faded, so did he.

I lost my train of thought as he attempted to grab me again. For the breadth of a moment I could swear one of his fingers grazed my wrist.

"*Nooo!*" he shouted as his image dimmed. He started to claw his arm again, while I tried desperately to jolt myself awake. Instead, I crash-landed somewhere unexpected. . . .

"Ladies, ladies, ladies, you're all smokin' hot. It's cruel to ask me to choose a winner."

Where was I? In the blink of an eye I went from nightmare to fantasy. I stood on South Beach, warm sand beneath my bare feet, crystalline water on the horizon, a purple-and-lime Art Deco lifeguard station to my left and an itsy-bitsy bikini on my bod.

Embarrassed, I tried to hike up my triangle top, but there wasn't much coverage to be had. I spun on my heel, looking for the source of this dreamscape.

What the—? Dan?

Sprawled on a beach lounger, sitting under a portable canopy, he looked toned and tan in a pair of red swim shorts. Not even his Maui Jims could hide the bliss on his face. Coulda been the picture-perfect weather, coulda been the icy cold microbrew in his cup holder, then again, it could have had something to do with the Miss Playa amateur bikini contestants surrounding him like a harem.

This guy didn't just escape from reality—he dream-vacationed in another universe.

Perturbed that he didn't let a little thing like, ohhh, a killer stalking us ruin his dreams,

I marched over to his oasis to . . . to . . . I don't know what.

"Dan!" I shouted from my spot behind the bevy of beauties.

"Hold up," he said and motioned for the girls to part. When he saw me, he raised his shades, scoped me out from top to toe, stopping for a while on another T-word, and then grinned maniacally. "I may have spoken too soon," he informed the contestants. "Perhaps we have a winner, after all."

My eyebrows shot up. A quick scan of the other girls' glowering faces told me I had heard him right. I pointed to myself, just to be sure. He answered with a sexy wink. My stomach swirled and I blushed with pleasure. Maybe there was something to be said about not *always* being invisible.

Perhaps it was the plethora of "Die, bitch" glares I had aimed at me, but my ego boost was short-lived. Facing off with Rafe in my last dream was terrifying, but being the target of murderous models gave me the willies. I scooted my way through Silicone Valley to have a private word with Dan.

"Do you think maybe we could be alone?" I whispered, keeping a careful eye on the scowls and stilettos at my back.

"Sure, Trin," he said, a presumptuous smile on his face.

I rolled my eyes, but a part of me also thrilled to his attention. No one had ever looked at me like that.

Per my request, Dan asked the girls to leave. They simpered and begged to stay, while baring their cat claws at me. *Me-ow!*

When the last pinup girl faded into the sun, Dan turned to me. "What can I do for you?" he asked in a sultry tone.

In reflex, my toes curled into the sand. *Oh, the ways I could answer that. . . .*

Despite serious temptation to play along, I asked, "What am I doing here?" I still had no clue how I'd ended up on Fantasy Island.

Dan frowned in confusion. "I thought you came to see me."

I did? Was that possible?

I looked around, wondering if this was

some kind of trick. Was Rafe orchestrating things? Then again, how could he when he was nowhere to be seen? Maybe Dan somehow pushed past him and entered my dreams like everyone else.

I thought about that for a minute. No. This little scenario didn't feel right. Usually my dreams were dark, moody, and bleak. Grisly reality. Dan's dream was happily delusional. He hadn't visited me. Had I really visited him?

"Whoa," I uttered, motioning first to my bikini, then to the cabana. "So, this is like one of your regular dreams?"

"I don't think I'm dreaming, but if I am, don't wake me. I want you here." He stepped closer and my breath hitched. "With me." I looked up into his eyes and got lost. Then he tried to take my hand in his and his fingers swept right through me.

Not fair. I wanted him to touch me.

I guess since I had cognizant awareness of being in his dream and he didn't, lucidity, and thereby physicality, eluded him. I could touch him, but he couldn't touch me. What a shame.

This sharing a dream with someone who wasn't lucid was a new sitch for me. It felt like snooping through someone's closet. What other good things did he have in here? And would he still have dreamed about me even if I hadn't popped in?

"Dan," I said softly, laying my hand on his chest, "there's nowhere I'd rather be."

"Is that true, now?" asked a familiar voice.

I stiffened as Robert Devlin, Dan's dad, strode into the cabana dressed in a charcoal Burberry golf shirt and canvas cap. He looked less like a cutthroat attorney than a poster boy for the rich and bored.

His arrival changed Dan's entire demeanor. Gone was the casual playboy who exuded confidence and fun, and in his place stood a withdrawn young man with shuttered eyes, a stony face, and don't-get-too-close-to-me posture.

"Why are you here?" Dan asked, stepping away from me.

Mr. Devlin gave his son a friendly slap on the shoulder. "Is that any way to treat your father, Dan boy?"

Dan narrowed his eyes, not answering the question.

Mr. Devlin didn't seem to notice. Instead he locked eyes with me.

"Who's this?" he asked.

Who's this?!? I opened my mouth, ready to tear him a new one, but Dan spoke first.

"You don't recognize her?" he asked in disgust.

Devlin Senior's gaze swept over me. "Should I?"

He spoke about me as if I wasn't standing right there hearing every word. I clenched my fists against the urge to slap him.

"That's Trinity," Dan snapped at his dad. He watched his father for a reaction. "Trinity *Michaels*," he nudged further.

Annnd there it was . . . Mr. Devlin jerked back. "Dream Girl?"

Recognition registered and he turned to his son, revulsion blotching his face. "Tell me you do not have a thing for *her*."

I froze and my gaze shot to Dan. Before he could answer, or I could blabber something to derail the uncomfortable conversation, Mr. Devlin cut in.

"That's unacceptable," he said. "She nearly cost me that case."

"By telling the truth," Dan gritted out.

"She's trouble."

"No, you are," Dan insisted.

Mr. Devlin laughed. "Don't go getting high and mighty," he said. "You won't get anywhere in life without breaking a few rules."

"You don't just break them, Dad." Dan spat out the last word like he had something vile in his mouth. "You crush them and anyone who gets in your way."

"You exaggerate," Mr. Devlin said, "and you have no right to complain. Look at the life I've given you."

Dan shook his head. "It's always the same thing with you . . . the end justifies the means. Well, I don't want my life to be about money. And I want a father I can respect."

"Everyone respects me," Mr. Devlin declared. "I demand it."

"You have no integrity," Dan said. "People

fear you, they do not respect you."

"Whatever pays the bills," his father replied blithely.

I flinched. I hated to bear witness to this private, and obviously oft-repeated, argument, but I couldn't exactly leave. It wasn't *my* dream. But it was just about all I could do not to step right up to Robert Devlin, Esquire, and tell him exactly what I thought of him. Then he put me over the edge.

"You're going nowhere fast." He sniffed at Dan. "Get off your high horse, already, and make something of yourself."

I lunged at him shouting, "Fu—"

Beep, beep, beep.

Startled, I looked around. What the—? Was I being censored in my own dream?

Beep, beep, beep, BEEP.

Saved by the hotel alarm clock.

Chapter 9

I woke up wrapped around Dan. Quickly, I reached across him, slapped off the alarm clock—mentally cursing the last person who had stayed here—and slumped back onto the sheets. Shoving hanks of hair out of my face, I stared up at him. He looked all sleep-mussed, whiskery, and sexy. Not to mention sound asleep. The boy hadn't budged. I sighed in relief and realized my cheek was planted on his bare chest and my legs were entwined with his.

And here I'd been the one to erect the pillow barrier between us! Talk about embarrassing. Slowly, and more reluctantly than I wanted to admit, I extricated my limbs from his.

Unbelievable. I had just slept with a guy.

Not in any kind of sexual way, but still. Lying under the covers now, feeling his body mere inches away, I thought about what it would be like. Sex, I mean. With Dan. The very idea made me squirm a little and I figured I'd better stop that line of thinking NOW.

I scooted a couple inches farther away and tugged the extra pillows out from beneath the covers (lot of good they had done) to prop up my shoulders. Any second now Dan would wake and I'd just have to pretend I hadn't cuddled against him or played Peeping Tomasina in his dream.

Remembering everything, I shut my eyes and sank farther into my pillows. No doubt about it, I had to keep last night's revelations secret.

I mean, what good would come of telling Dan about Rafe? What would I even say? "Why, I do believe his reception came in clearer when he mutilated himself." Ha! Dan would admit *me* into the psych hospital. Besides I really didn't know what to make of my warped meeting of the minds with Rafe. He couldn't possibly have touched me.

Could he have?

A shiver jetted through me and I hugged the covers close. I felt—what was the phrase Dan had used?—*intruded upon*. The idea that someone could hurt me through my own dreams was incomprehensible. And terrifying.

As for Dan's beach-babes-gone-wrong dream, I thought it best to pretend it didn't happen. Acknowledging that we were both attracted to each other would only complicate things—and I'd just about had it with complications. Then, too, I didn't want to embarrass him by telling him I'd witnessed his father's verbal abuse. Besides, Dan might take offense to my, er, "stopping by," and there was enough tension between us already without me breaking and entering his dreams.

Never, ever, had I hopped into someone's dream before. Yet all I'd done was *touch* Dan. It's not like I hadn't rolled against someone in bed before—my mom, sleepovers with Coral—but nothing like this had ever happened.

So why Dan?

Did it mean he was evil like Rafe?

Or did it mean there was something deeper between Dan and me? Some kind of—dare I think it—soul-mate connection?

Either answer left me scared.

But fear feathered away when I heard a husky "Good morning" next to me.

I rolled on my side to face him. "Hi," I said, almost shyly.

He scrubbed at his eyes and gave me a lop-sided grin. "I've never woken up next to some-one before."

I hadn't expected that little confession, but I was glad to hear it. "Me, neither. And I haven't slept next to a snorer, either."

He lifted an eyebrow. "I don't know who you were sleeping next to. I don't snore."

I giggled. "Keep telling yourself that."

"Well, at least I didn't breach the pillow barrier," he said with a smug smile.

I gasped and then buried my face in my pillow. I didn't know if I was more embarrassed that he knew I'd put up a barrier or that I'd crawled over it and cuddled up against him.

"Sorry," I murmured into the pillow.

He chuckled. "Trust me, it was no prob."

I looked up and caught his teasing look. Whoa, now he was flirting with me *outside* his dreams.

"It was totally involuntary, you know," I said.

"Uh-huh. I *totally* believe you," he said, a mocking "suuure it was" attitude in his tone. "But I liked it just the same."

I bit my lip to keep from saying something stupid, like, "Me, too."

Then I jerked my gaze to his as something occurred to me. "Did you, uh, have good dreams?"

"Yeah, a mix of good"—he smiled, as if suddenly remembering me in my bikini—"*really* good and bad. You?"

"Same, er, I mean"—I broke eye contact—"I don't really remember."

Thankfully, he didn't clue into my guilt.

"At least you didn't dream about Rafe," he said, flipping back the covers. "How 'bout we go find him before he finds you?"

"Sounds like a plan," I agreed, but then wondered if it wasn't too late.

Life's a beach and then you die.

Isn't that how the saying goes? It certainly seemed to fit my life right now. At the rate things were going, Rafe was sure to find me before I found him.

Dan and I had spent that morning snooping around Rafe's hangouts and getting nowhere fast. We were trying to track a killer—along with the entire STATE, which had been alerted to Rafe's AWOL status—and still there was no sign of him. Dead ends, slammed doors, and tight lips led to frustration. Dan must've sensed my mood.

"This sucks."

"You could say that," I agreed.

He curved his arm around my waist. "How 'bout I take you to lunch?" he offered. "You look ready for a break."

Startled, I looked up at him. Any other time

that sentence could be construed as a date request, but I didn't think that applied here. Did it?

"I'd like that," I said, nervously toying with the end of my ponytail.

Together we walked to the nearby News Café at 8th & Ocean Drive. Dan pulled out a chair for me at one of their round patio tables. The gentlemanly move certainly made me *feel* like I was on a date.

Despite the wood-backed chairs not being especially comfortable, I let out an audible sigh. It felt soooo good to get off my feet and shuck my backpack. My black-and-pink-checked Vans might be sweet, but they weren't the best walking shoes. At least I'd packed a pair of cute black cargo shorts and a hot-pink tank with black lace trim. Sitting under a hunter-green umbrella, we perused the menu. Although I'd eaten here previously I still flinched when I read, "Grilled dolphin sandwich."

"Poor Flipper," I murmured, as I had every time before.

"You do know that's a dolphin *fish* sandwich

and not the dolphin mammal, right?"

"Says you."

He chuckled. "Says the law."

"In my heart I know it's not really Flipper, but I just can't eat something with the same name."

"Would you mind if I ordered it?" Dan asked with a playful glint in his eyes.

I wrinkled my nose in distaste but didn't know how to answer. Fortunately he let me off the hook with a wink.

"I'm just razzing you. I don't want it and I really don't want to give you more nightmares."

"Why, thank you, sir, I do appreciate your kindness," I drawled like some syrupy southern belle. Then I leaned closer and studied his incredible blue eyes, made all the bluer by his T-shirt. "Seriously. Have you really eaten"—gulp!—"dolphin?"

With an inscrutable poker face he asked, "You want the truth?"

I shook my head. "Maybe not."

Just then, his serious expression melted into a soft and silly smile. My heart hammered in response. This guy here, unguarded and unconcerned for a moment about his dad or danger, was a real threat to me. He was the kind of guy I could find myself falling for. He was—

"I could never eat Flipper," he told me, interrupting my derailed thoughts. "It would be worse than eating Bambi."

I slumped back in my chair, but I wasn't sure if I was relieved over his sparing the dolphin or me snapping out of my Dan-induced daze.

When the waiter came I readily gave in to the distraction and ordered a soft-shell crab sandwich, while Dan requested a Philly cheesesteak. Since I'd already established that I wasn't a "grazer," there was no sense in doing something girly like ordering a salad. Good thing, too; I was famished.

"I think we'll feel better after we eat," Dan told me.

"I just hope they hurry." Looking at him, I said something I'd been thinking about all day. "You'd make a good detective. It suits you."

He raised his eyebrows. "Really? Should I

get a fedora"—he tipped the rim of an imaginary hat at me—"and maybe a trench coat? We could be like Dick Tracy and Tess Trueheart."

"I don't know about comics, but I love nineteen forties film noir," I said wistfully. "It's so sexy."

"Yeah?"

Mmmhmm," I hummed, drawn into the fantasy. "Manly men, sexy stockings, and raw passion." Seeing Dan's eyes suddenly darken, I took a sip of ice water to cool myself down.

"I see your point," he said. "And I'm looking at the forties with a whole new appreciation."

My cheeks warmed. "Yeah, well," I said, a bit self-consciously, "you seriously have a knack for following bread crumbs."

"Thanks, but the crumby trail didn't lead us anywhere."

I shrugged. "No, but it tells us where he's not."

We sat quietly then, lost in our own thoughts. I concentrated on pushing fantasies of Dan in a dark suit and fedora out of my brain and instead soaked in my surroundings. Traffic on Ocean was light, leaving a good view of the gorgeous greenbelt across the street. Palm trees swayed like rhythmic hula dancers in grass skirts, and the unblemished azure sky made me hope one day I wouldn't always have some kind of emotional rain cloud hanging over my head. Maybe one day I would sit here and actually know whether or not I was on a real date.

When the waiter set down our food, the tangy ocean scent I'd been appreciating was replaced with the smell of hot Cajun fries. I immediately snatched one off my plate and then moaned in pleasure at the crispy spiciness.

"You have to have one," I told Dan. "They're sooo good."

I held one up to his mouth and when he took a bite, his lips grazed my finger. My gaze jumped to his and we got locked in to a sizzling staredown. Suddenly, the hot fries weren't the only thing generating heat.

"*Mmm,*" Dan said. "Delish."

I lowered my gaze and my hand. "*Hmm,* yeah, so what were we talking about?"

"Rafe. Let's go over what we do know about him." Dan took a big bite of his sandwich and chewed thoughtfully before speaking. "He's not at his home or any of his usual hang-outs, neighbors said they never saw him with a girlfriend, and we can't find Dr. Erskine."

"Yet," I said with a point of my fork. "But we need to keep trying. As Rafe's shrink he should have more ideas than anyone about his whereabouts."

"You'd think," Dan agreed. "Unless he's just some hack my dad's got in his back pocket."

I narrowed my eyes. "What do you mean?"

"I mean, maybe he's some crony who'd do anything Dad told him to and the guy never bothered to evaluate Rafe."

I felt my crab sandwich skitter in my stomach.

"You really think—?"

"I really think my dad's capable of anything," he said grimly.

"Maybe he is," I said. I mean, who was I to argue? If his own son thought he was completely devoid of any morality, that said a lot about his character. "Then the real question becomes: Is Dr. Erskine capable of that kind of deceit?"

"He's the key, isn't he?" Dan said softly, then shook his head. "Trin, I'm sorry this hasn't gone easier, but don't give up on me."

"Give up on *you*?" I repeated in shock. "If I didn't have you—" I cut myself off before I said too much. "I'm just glad I have someone on my side. Erskine is our best lead. We'll start there."

"You think the police and press are doing any better?" Dan asked.

We'd kept the truck's radio on during our earlier investigation, but news reports had been more dramatized than detailed. "Beware—dangerous, psychotic child killer on the loose." I could just envision mothers everywhere locking their daughters indoors, while the media foamed at the mouth for ways to further sensationalize the story.

I scooted back my chair. "I don't know. I'll check the newsstand and see if there's any info."

"Good thinking," Dan said and pulled his

wallet from the back pocket of his shorts. "I'll wait here."

I hesitated, not sure if I should offer my share of the bill since I didn't know if this was a date or not.

"Go ahead," Dan said, seeing me pause. "It's my treat."

"You sure?" I asked, awkward and unsure.

"Positive. You can catch the next one, if you want."

"Okay," I readily agreed. "It's a date." Oops! Had I said the D-word out loud? I was ready to bolt when Dan grinned and said, "You know where to pick me up."

I matched his grin and headed inside the newsstand, where I overanalyzed whether we had already been on a date or just made plans for one. The whole thing was clear as mud.

News about Rafe wasn't any more crystal. All the papers had his mug shot on the front page but no real leads to his whereabouts.

Of course, why would he have to go anywhere if he could reach his victim in her sleep?

I tripped and bumped into a rack.

He can't harm me, I assured myself. *He cannot harm me in my sleep.*

I bought some gum to work off my nervous energy. It kept me from biting my nails, and it's always good when you can talk or chew yourself out of hysteria.

Darn my susceptible nature. If you even put a suggestion of something in my head—like, oh, say those severe allergy warnings on medicine labels—I'm bound to convince myself that's what's happening to me. The very idea of murder by psyche was laughable. How could I even entertain something so nutty? I couldn't. Not unless I was completely ridorkulous—and I wasn't.

Feeling better, I headed out to the patio.

Dan's back faced me, but I could see he was talking on his cell phone. Was this the same "friend" he'd called before? Curious, I took a few steps closer, intending to sit at the table while he finished his conversation, but something in his low tone raised the hackles on my neck. I froze four paces behind him and listened.

"So far she hasn't been much help," Dan said.

Was he talking about me?

"No, far as I know, she hasn't dreamed about him."

He was!

"I'm doing everything I can. Have you got any more leads? No. We're going to try Erskine again. I think he's the key."

Something about the tenor of this conversation set off warning sirens. *A-oo-gah! A-oo-gah!*

"Yes, her, too. Don't worry, I think we'll get what we need."

He listened intently for a moment and then said, "C'mon. What do you want me to do with her? It doesn't work that way. Hold off. I promised to help you and I will, but you need to do your part, too."

Oh my God, what was he talking about? What was he supposed to do to me? Had Dan been using me all along? Who was he helping? His dad? Rafe? My head went tingly as fear coursed through me. Instinctually, I backed up to escape. My legs collided with a chair, making it screech across the concrete. Dan whirled around and, seeing my stricken face, slammed his phone shut.

"Trinity," he said, rising from his chair, his arms raised in a placating manner. "It's not what it sounded like."

I didn't say a word, I just whirled and ran.

Chapter 10

A primo Ford Shelby GT convertible with Vista Blue paint and silver stripes missed me by mere inches.

I braced my hands on its hood and the driver, a mid-life-crisis gigolo, opened his door to see if I was okay. Before I could assure him I was, Dan shouted my name too close for comfort. Without looking, I dashed the rest of the way across Ocean Drive.

"Trinity!" he yelled again, weaving around honking cars.

I ran across a stretch of grass and hit the boardwalk, then the beach.

Too late, I realized my dumb mistake.

As soon as I hit the sand my slip-on shoes

filled up. Before I could kick them off and bolt on bare feet, Dan had grabbed hold of my backpack and spun me around.

"Please let me explain," he huffed.

I wrenched away from him, trembling in anger and fear. "'What do you want me to *do* with her?'" I repeated his frightening words.

He flinched. "It's not the way it sounds."

"Really?" I gave him a doubtful look, then yanked off my shoes so I could make a quick getaway. "Why should I believe you?"

"Because I'm the only one trying to help you."

"Are you?" I shoved his chest hard, making him stumble backward. "Seems to me you're trying to help someone else."

"I'm here to keep you safe," he said, righting himself.

"And what else?" I demanded.

"And . . ."

His voice faltered and I thought for sure he was making up some b.s. story on the spot.

"And, I'm trying to get dirt on my dad so I can have him disbarred."

Not bad for b.s. It actually had the ring of truth to it, but I wasn't easily convinced. "How could you do that?" I asked, narrowing my eyes at him.

"By giving information to Alan Kelley."

I knew the name, but why? "Who's he?"

"A prosecutor."

"Prosecutor?" I frowned. "So that makes him your dad's nemesis."

"You could say that."

I whacked him on the shoulder with one of my shoes. "This isn't about keeping me safe, it's about exacting revenge on your dad?"

"No." He held up his arms to stave off any more blows. "I don't want you hurt, Trin," he said quietly. "I don't want anyone hurt."

I lowered my shoe.

He stepped closer and cupped my shoulders. "I really do want to protect you."

I shrugged away from him. "That might be true, but you want to nail your dad to the frickin' wall and you're willing to use me to do it. You think I'm some sort of psychic bloodhound, don't you?"

His silence confirmed my suspicion.

"I'm not a human lie detector, Dan," I said wearily. "I've told you my abilities don't work like that. I'm not suddenly going to have some kind of 'vision' about what happened between your dad and Rafe. I don't read minds. And I don't get precognitive flashes."

"I know. I know," he said, obviously in an effort to placate me. "I get that, Trin. That's what I was telling Alan. There's nothing I can do to 'make' you dream about Rafe. But you have dreamed about him before and—"

I ducked my gaze, not wanting him to see in my eyes that Rafe had dropped by last night, but my not-so-subtle gesture gave me away.

"You dreamed about him again, didn't you?" he asked in an incredulous tone. "Why didn't you tell me? What happened?"

"Nothing," I said, dismissing his questions.

"If it was *nothing*," he spat the word, "you wouldn't have kept it a secret. What're you hiding?"

"Me?" I asked in outrage. "I'm not the one

hiding things and *using* people."

"Right," he scoffed. "You've been using me since day one. My name opens doors for you, and if I can help you find Rafe it will soothe your guilt over Kiri's death."

I felt like he'd punched me in the stomach.

"That's not true—"

He pointed an accusing finger at me. "You blame yourself and you're trying to make amends."

"How dare you!" I shouted. A few nearby sunbathers stared at us and I lowered my voice. "You have no idea what it's like to be me. I suppose you think you could learn people's deepest, darkest secrets and know just what to do with them, don't you?"

He folded his arms over his chest. "I sure as hell wouldn't turn my back on anyone," he said in a cold voice.

"Is that right?" I asked, dumbfounded by the way Dan seemed to know all my weaknesses. "Is that because of your 'high-and-mighty' morals?"

He stepped back and eyed me with suspicion.

"What's the matter, 'Dan boy'?"

His mouth thinned to a hard line.

"Say something," I demanded. "Or is it true 'you're going nowhere fast'?"

"How'd you—?"

"See!" I cried. "It's the ugly stuff I learn in my dreams."

"You were in my head," he accused.

"And you want inside *my* head." I tapped my temple. "You want to use me. To use a part of me I can't stand."

"I could say the same for you," he sneered. "You're using my dad's name to get what you want."

"Enough." I held up my hands and took two steps back. "You're right. I used you and now I'm done with you."

I walked away, shoes in hand, heart in throat.

"Trinity, wait," he said. "Don't go."

I kept walking.

"Trinity!" he shouted. "Do you really think you can survive on your own?"

"I'll have to," I said to myself without looking back.

I'll admit I wanted him to come after me. But he didn't.

So I walked around aimlessly before settling on an empty playground on the greenbelt. There I bawled my eyes out with loud snuffling sobs until the only thing left was hiccups for air. I didn't know what to do or where to go. I'd tried calling my mom, but her phone had gone straight to voice mail. Chances were she was in a museum and had turned it off. I thought about leaving a message, but anything I might've said would've spun her into a panic.

Feeling disconnected and scared, I swung my pack over one shoulder, walked back to Ocean Drive, and hailed a taxi. It seemed to me there was only one person who might be able to give me answers.

"Where to?" the cabbie asked.

"Nevaeh, city cemetery."

Cemeteries are funny places.

Their manicured lawns are gorgeous and

there's a serene quietness that humbles the soul, but one loud noise and I'm ready to jump out of my skin.

Now, as I walked to Kiri's grave, I tried to still my stomach's nervous quaking. What did I think? That she'd thrust her hand up through the dirt *à la Carrie*? I walked around the hedgerow that led to Kiri's plot. I hadn't been there since the funeral, a year ago, but I felt the need to visit with her now.

And I don't mean visit in the "I see dead people" sense.

I planned to talk to her in the same way anyone visiting a grave does. It was selfish, really. Dan had hit a nerve when he'd mentioned my guilt over Kiri's death, and I needed to talk to her, to pull myself together. I didn't really expect her to talk back. I know I had to find the answers deep within myself, but maybe, just maybe, her spirit would guide me.

What I didn't expect was to find someone else seeking Kiri's counsel.

He gripped her tombstone with both hands, his head bowed in heavy reverence. He made an awful keening sound, and my eyes watered in sympathy. I was torn about whether to leave him in peace or reach out to comfort him. Then he lifted his head, as if sensing my presence, and looked directly at me.

"I'm so-sorry," I stammered. Feeling guilty for having intruded, I pivoted on my heel to leave. "I'll come back," I said.

"Wait," he cried, his voice raw from sobbing. "I know you, don't I?"

I turned and walked toward him, expecting to see a familiar family member or friend of Kiri's. He was neither.

"Dr. Erskine?"

He was almost unrecognizable, with his scruffy salt-and-pepper beard and well-wrinkled clothes, but I knew this was the man who'd sworn under oath that Rafe Stevens was clinically insane. He'd claimed Rafe was schizophrenic and suffered from auditory hallucinations, and therefore could not be held criminally liable for his heinous crimes.

He'd lied.

Dr. Erskine wiped at his swollen eyes and

squinted at me for a better look.

"It's you. You're the girl who dreamed about Kiri," he said with remorse.

I nodded. At least he hadn't called me Dream Girl.

"Rafe's escaped," he blurted and then braced himself as if he were expecting me to dole out his punishment.

"Yeah, I know," I said, probably sounding more unaffected than I really was.

His face registered surprise and then, "Is that why you're here?"

"You could say that." I wasn't going to offer this man any of my personal deets.

He scurried around the pink marble tombstone to stand before me, wringing his hands. "You have to hide. Stay out of sight. Go somewhere safe," he directed with great urgency.

"I'm doing my best to stay safe," I assured him, "but I need to find Rafe before he finds me."

"No, no, no," he jibbered, "you can't do that. Leave that to the authorities. You must disappear until he's caught."

"That could be never. The guy's got skills.

He's disappeared like the invisible man."

"He'll kill again," Erskine declared. "And you're on the top of his list."

Tell me something I don't know.

"Did he tell you I'm his number-one victim?" I asked. "Because, you know, you can't always trust a schizophrenic."

Erskine blanched and looked around the cemetery.

When he seemed sure no one living, or dead, was listening, he said, "He's evil and depraved, but he's not schizophrenic."

"Not schizo?" I parroted in faux shock.

Erskine had the decency to look ashamed. "No, I know that's what I said in court"—he held up his hand when I opened my mouth—"but it's not true. Rafe's actually a sociopath. He's the type who could lie through his teeth on a polygraph and still pass because he shows no remorse."

"And why the hell didn't you say that in court?" I demanded.

"Because sociopaths can't be found criminally insane," he explained. "They know the difference between right and wrong. They just don't care."

"So you testified that he was schizo to give him a 'Get Out of Jail Free' card."

"I, I didn't want to, but then Robert Devlin . . ."

"Persuaded you," I prompted.

"Yes." He shielded his face with his hands, but he couldn't hide his shame.

I grabbed his wrists and uncovered his face, which was wet with tears. "He bribed you, didn't he?"

Dr. Erskine shook his head fiercely. "Oh, no, Robert Devlin would never do anything as vulgar as bribery," he said, his voice venomous with sarcasm. "Instead, he approached me as if he were doing *me* a favor. Only later did I realize his perfect conviction record had been threatened and he was willing to do anything to stop that."

"How much?" I asked.

He grimaced before answering. "Fifty K." The doctor wouldn't meet my eyes. "You have to believe I've never lied before. But, I . . . I had some gambling debts. It's no excuse, I just figured Rafe would still be locked up, so what was the harm?"

"Then what?" I asked in a flat voice.

"Then I heard Rafe had escaped. It made me realize what I'd done and—I'm ashamed to admit this—I thought about Kiri for the first time. I never considered the impact of my testimony on her family. On anyone, other than me."

I didn't know what to say. But somewhere along the line my anger with this man had turned to pity.

"If he kills someone again because of my testimony"—his voice cracked with emotion—"I couldn't live with myself." He laid a weathered hand on the top of Kiri's tombstone. "I came here to apologize, to ask for her forgiveness, and to tell her I wanted to make things right in any way I could." He looked at me, eyes sharp and intent. "Now I believe she brought you here. To me."

Whoa. I hadn't thought about that. But I'd

been looking in vain for him and here he was. Maybe—

"You want to make things right?" I interrupted my own thoughts.

"Yes," he said with conviction. "For me and for Kiri."

"Then tell the truth," I implored.

His ruddy complexion paled. "I'll lose my job."

"You might," I agreed, "but would that be worse than feeling like an accessory to Kiri's murder for the rest of your life?"

Erskine seemed to consider the alternative. "What about Robert Devlin?" he asked pointedly.

"He's sure to lose his job," I said.

"That, right there," Erskine said in a steely tone, "is enough reason for me to confess."

Karma seemed to be catching up quickly with Robert Devlin.

"He was wrong to play on your addiction," I told Erskine.

He grimaced in pain. "I wonder how many

other criminals he's helped put back on the streets."

"Good question," I said, disturbed by the thought. "Maybe he's no better than the people he defends."

"Of that I have no doubt." Erksine stepped closer to me. "So tell me about your plan."

My plan? My plan was to stay alive, pure and simple.

"Umm."

"First we have to take you someplace safe," he said. "You can stay with me."

I shook my head. "No, thank you. Someone is already looking after me."

"Are you sure I can't help?" the doctor asked. "I feel responsible."

I gave an inelegant snort and covered it up with a cough. I'd heard those very words before and it didn't instill a sense of trust in me. "You can help by testifying, but first we need to get Rafe. Do you have any idea where he might be?"

I could see him hesitate, unsure whether or

not I was ready for the whole truth. Then he trusted me with it. "I talked to Rafe enough to know he's truly depraved, but I never did an actual assessment. I wish I knew enough to help you find him, but I don't."

I slumped.

"Have you checked with Robert Devlin?" Erskine asked. "After all, he was the guy who coached Rafe. He might know something."

"What do you mean, he coached him?" I stammered.

"Robert knew Rafe played crazy on the scene and he *advised*"—he made sarcastic air quotes showing his derision—"him to play that up."

Fraud. Bribery. Conspiracy. My mind ticked off the charges that could be pressed against Mr. Devlin.

Oh, yeah. Dan could get his dad, and good. Shock rippled through me. I couldn't imagine how Dan would feel when he learned the dirty truth. But, in the meantime, I still had to find a killer before he found me.

"We'll see if Mr. Devlin knows anything," I told Erskine, "and I'll leave your name out of it, but I need your word that when this ends"—*however that might be*—"you'll testify against him."

"I swear on Kiri's grave," he said earnestly.

It was a promise I knew he'd keep.

As Erskine drifted away, I finally had the moment alone with Kiri that I'd come for. The smell of fresh-mowed grass tickled my nostrils. I leaned my back against the sun-warmed tombstone and stretched out my legs. A quiet comfort stole over me and I let it embrace me.

"Thank you," I told her. I, too, believed she'd orchestrated this meeting. "I will see that the truth comes out. I owe you that." I hung my head and felt the tears begin. Dan had been right. I did feel guilty about Kiri's death. Logically, I knew it wasn't my fault that the police had arrived too late to save her. I'd done all that I could. But there had been so many times in the past when I hadn't. When Kiri reached out to me, begging me to save her, it was my chance to make up for all the times I'd turned away.

And she was gone.

Had others slipped away because of me? Because I was too indifferent, too unaffected, too damned stubborn to own my abilities?

Kiri's death, more than anything, had forced me to examine who I was. And I didn't like what I saw.

"I've failed myself most of all," I whispered brokenly.

A gentle breeze stroked my hair like a caress.

"I'll do better," I promised. And I had to start with the one person I knew I could help. Dan.

Chapter 11

"So, tell me what you know."

I latched my seat belt and gave Dan a droll look. "I'm happy to see you, too. Thanks for picking me up."

Ignoring my sarcasm he bullied forth. "You told me on the phone you had important news."

"No," I said tartly, "what I said was 'Can you come pick me up? I'm at the cemetery.' And you said, 'Picking out your plot?'"

He grimaced. "I was still pissed."

I rolled my eyes and smirked at him. "Gee, I couldn't tell."

"But you did say you knew something," he said. "You spoke with Erskine?"

"I did and I do." I settled into my seat, folding

my arms over my chest and looking straight through the dirty windshield. Dan would have to wait for further details; I wasn't quite ready to show him all my cards. "Let's get out of here," I insisted.

The gravestones looked longer in dusk's shadows. I shivered, glad to leave the dead as darkness came.

"Come on, Trinity," Dan growled as he started the truck and flipped on the headlights. "I don't want to play games."

I glanced at him. His hands were gripping the wheel tightly and his brow was furrowed. Maybe he was ashamed of lying to me. "I'm sorry," I told him, meaning it.

He gave me a dubious look. "For what?"

"For running away earlier. I do need you. And I really am glad to see you."

His tense shoulders lowered a fraction and his face relaxed. The doubt had left his eyes. "Ditto," he said. "Please don't take off like that again, I was really worried about you. I know the call sounded bad, but—"

"It doesn't matter anymore," I interrupted,

wanting to move past this tension between us, "because I have what it takes to put your dad away. We need to be a team on this." I turned in my seat to face him. "I have to trust you and you have to trust me."

A kaleidoscope of emotions shifted across his face—shock, excitement, regret.

"What do you know?" he asked with trepidation.

"Uh-uh." I shook my head. "I can't tell you just yet." He opened his mouth to object, but I cut him off, pressing my finger to his lips. "You've compromised my trust. If I tell you everything, who's to say you won't abandon me and go running off to Kelley?" I kept my tone light, but I was hoping he'd reassure me.

"You're the one who ran off on me. And didn't you just say we have to trust each other?" Dan pointed out.

"True, but I'm not the one with ulterior motives and an outside contact. I need you to be with me on this to the end." Ugh, "the end" sounded so final.

Dan matched my careful tone as he pulled

out of the cemetery. "And how do I know you aren't jerking me around?"

I pulled Erskine's business card from my backpack. I'd caught up with the doctor before leaving the cemetery and asked for it, and explained to him who my ally was. To say he'd been surprised would be an understatement, but I also think he took some perverse delight in knowing it was Devlin's own son who'd take him down. The doctor had scribbled his cell phone number on the back of the card without hesitation.

Taking one hand off the wheel, Dan took the card and looked it over. Setting it on the seat between us, he shrugged. "So he gave you his card. That doesn't mean he told you anything."

My jaw dropped. What a hard-ass! "Why else would he give me his personal number?"

"Maybe you lifted it off him," he countered, nodding back toward the cemetery. "Maybe he dropped it in the graveyard."

"Come on," I laughed. He was grasping at straws and he knew it. "I've been up front with you from the start, admitting on day one why I needed you. You have no reason *not* to trust me."

"You didn't tell me about your dream," he murmured.

"Because there really wasn't anything to tell," I said in aggravation. "Rafe threatened me. End of dream."

"And how'd you know so much about me?" he challenged.

I winced. "I honestly don't know how I ended up in your dream. I'm sorry about that. I think it's because we touched"—my gaze flitted to his and then away—"er, bumped into each other while we were sleeping."

The quick way he looked at me, then looked away, told me this little tidbit startled him. "Has that ever happened to you before?"

"Nope," I admitted. "Guess this was a total fluke."

He worked his jaw back and forth, clearly a little unnerved.

"What else did you see in my dream?"

"A softer, goofier side of you. I saw—"

"You in a bikini?"

"Yeah," I said with a smile, "along with a bevy of other girls."

"I can only remember a little. But I remember you." He looked at me intently. "Us."

"And then your dad showed up."

He nodded. "Leave it to him to ruin everything."

"I'm sorry I invaded your privacy," I said softly. "It wasn't on purpose."

"I know."

"You should also know you were right," I offered.

"About?"

I was about to make myself vulnerable. Did I want to do that? Well, if you can't confide in someone with whom you share MORTAL DANGER, who can you confide in?

Taking a deep breath, I said, "I do feel guilty. Not so much about Kiri's death, but because she represents the cries for help that I ignored."

He didn't say anything for a moment and

then, "You can't be expected to right everyone's wrongs."

The knot in my stomach unclenched.

He looked me in the eye and in a contrite tone said, "I was a real ass to say you turned your back on people. I can only imagine how rough things must be sometimes for you."

"Thank you," I said, his empathy easing my guilt. "But I know I could've done more."

He reached out and gave my hand a quick squeeze. "Then you will now."

I nodded and hoped the evening's shadows hid my regret-filled tears.

"All right," he said as we headed back toward SoBe. "So we're in this together. Did Erskine have any ideas?"

"Your dad." I watched Dan's knuckles whiten on the wheel. "He spoke to Rafe more than anyone."

Dan grimaced in acknowledgment. "I already called him."

Now it was my turn to be shocked. "Wow, you must've been desperate."

"Yeah, well, other than chewing me out for taking off, he said he had 'no friggin' clue' and I'd better not be playing 'super sleuth.'"

I frowned. "You didn't tell him you were looking?"

"No. And I didn't tell him you were with me, either."

I nodded. "You know, it's been a looong day. What do you say we get something to eat and call it a night?"

"I'm always up for food," he admitted.

I smiled but didn't say anything.

"You okay?" he asked with concern.

"Tired, maybe a little shaken."

"Maybe?" Dan repeated doubtfully.

I quirked my mouth to the side. "Okay, definitely. Guess I'm a little raw right now."

"I may be able to help," he offered. "What you need is a nice, plush hotel room and a little pampering."

"That sounds nice," I said, "but I can't ask you to do that. I still owe you for last night's rate."

"No," Dan argued. "We're going to the

Swaying Palms Resort Hotel and I'm charging it to dear old Daddy's card. It's the least he could do. Tonight you'll be in the lap of luxury."

Superstitiously, I crossed my fingers and wished for sweet dreams.

I should have known better.

Never in my life had I been more comfortable. A plump down pillow, expensive high-thread-count sheets, and a mattress that felt like a fresh marshmallow.

Plush perfection.

And I could *not* go to sleep.

Exhaustion made me physically ache, but my brain refused to say, "Night-night." My earlier fight with Dan, the encounter with Erskine, and my emotional revelation about my ability had all taken a toll on me. Tears came quick and easy.

"Hey, now," Dan soothed, hearing me cry. He rolled toward me and stroked my back. "What's the matter?"

"You've pampered me like a princess"—I snuffled—"with room service, a five-star hotel, and this amazing bed, and I can't even sleep." *Sniff, sniff.*

"It's been a stressful day," he said sympathetically. "You just need to relax."

"I can't," I practically wailed. "My mind's in overdrive. I keep thinking about Rafe, Kiri, my mom, your dad, Erskine, the future—"

"The future?"

"Will I have one?"

"Of course you will," he insisted.

"Dreams, you, Coral," I continued to recite.

"No wonder you can't sleep," he interrupted.

His hand settled into the curve of my hip and I startled at his touch.

"Trust me," he said, pulling me into his arms, spooning me with his warmth.

I won't lie. He felt even more heavenly than the bed.

"Dan, I—"

"I just want to hold you," he whispered.

"You can't," I said, more than a little sadly.

"If we both fall asleep I might hijack your dreams again."

He was quiet for a moment and then he promised, "I won't fall asleep until you do and then I'll scoot back to my own side."

"You don't have—"

"I want to. Now close your eyes and listen to my voice."

I snuggled back a little farther and closed my eyes.

"Imagine a perfect setting."

"The beach," I said, "at sunset."

"Perfect. Picture it in your mind. The sound, the smell, the taste, the feel."

I imagined it. Lapping waves on the shore, a spectacular sunset of pink and orange, a light breeze that carried the salty smell of the ocean, and me sitting on a checkered blanket with Dan watching the sun slowly dissolve into the watery horizon.

"Now let yourself be carried into that moment, like the gentle rhythmic waves," Dan instructed.

I started to float away.

He smoothed my hair and whispered. "I'll be with you."

I melted farther into his arms and slept.

Hours later I woke up screaming.

Panic drove me out of our bed. "I need to get out of here," I told Dan in wide-eyed agitation. My nerves were jangly and my skin felt flushed and tingly. "Now!"

"Okay, okay," he agreed, yanking on his jeans and a snug black tee. He gave the dress I'd thrown on a dubious look. "What do you have in mind?"

I looked down at *the* dress. I didn't know what I had in mind, only that I needed to get away, that I needed to *be*.

"Take me to Magia," I demanded.

Dan looked at me like I was off my rocker, and maybe I was, but he didn't argue. On the drive over he pressed me for details.

"It was Rafe," I said through gritted teeth. "Live. In person. We're talking three-dimensional, surround sound, smell-o-vision, digital clarity reception." I looked at Dan and knew he saw fear in my eyes. "Milt wasn't so wacko after all."

"Did Rafe do anything to you?" Dan asked urgently.

I shook my head, but wrapped my arms around myself to contain the trembles that wouldn't stop. "He didn't hurt me, but he whispered in my ear and I—" My fingers crept up to my right ear. "His breath actually stirred my hair."

"What did he say?"

I tried to answer but couldn't.

"Trin?" he softly prodded.

"He said"—I swallowed hard—"'You're gonna die before you wake.'"

"Sonofabitch!" Dan pounded the steering wheel. "But he didn't touch you?" he insisted.

"No."

He sat back a little. "Then he probably can't. Are you"—he gave me a wary look—"sure it wasn't just a bad dream? You were really worked up before you fell asleep."

"It was real!" I swore. "I could *smell* his blood."

Dan jerked the wheel and then straightened out. "Blood?"

"He was cutting his arm."

"What? So Rafe's into self-mutilation?" Dan asked. "But that's just—"

"Crazy," I supplied. "Only he's not cutting as a cry for help. Harming himself fuels his power. I think when Dr. Wrens tortured him it altered Rafe's brain like Milt said. It stretched instead of snapped. Now Rafe can't use his powers unless he's in pain."

"I can't believe—" Dan shook his head as if unable to conceptualize something that went against all logic. "And he really hurt himself that bad?"

I shuddered at the memory and Dan gripped my hand. "Dan," I said, squeezing him back, "it looked like he'd razored the rungs of a ladder right up his arm."

"Sweet Jesus," he swore. "Rafe's seriously bent."

I clenched my eyes shut, trying to block out the memory.

"I don't want to remember," I said. "I don't want any of this," I cried desperately. "Why

178

does any of this have to be a part of my life?"

Dan pulled into the parking lot and before he'd fully stopped I'd opened my door. A pulsing Latin beat thrummed through the air, and I knew I'd come to the right place.

Here, I could lose myself.

"Come on." I grabbed Dan's hand and pulled him after me.

Magia, which means magic in Spanish, was an open-air club that writhed with music and bodies fueled by margaritas and mojitos. I'd heard about the place but never checked it out. Tiny fairy lights decorated palm trees and color-lit waterfalls misted hedonistic dancers. The atmosphere crackled with passion and liberation.

I intended to dance away my demons.

Finding a spot near the waterfall, I closed my eyes and absorbed the tempo. I let it move me without inhibition or fear. Bunching the sides of my skirt in my hands, I lifted the hem higher and swished the material to the beat. Then I smoothed my hands over my hair and down my body. I became one with the music. I was a siren singing her seductive song, a temptress in the eye of a tempest, and when I opened my eyes I saw I'd ensnared Dan. He stood two feet away, his eyes piercing, hot. He liked what he saw. He liked *me*. Feeling bold, I laid my hands on his chest and undulated a circle around him. "Dance with me," I whispered in a sultry voice.

"Trin—"

A waiter breezed by with a tray of margaritas and I snagged one.

"Hey!" he snapped, but before he could card me or kick me out, Dan yanked a twenty from his wallet and handed it to the guy with an apology.

"No prob, dude," he said, pocketing the money.

I gave Dan an impish smile, then licked a spot of salt off the glass before taking a long sip through the straw. "Mmm"—I licked my lips—"yummy. Want some?"

Dan raised his eyebrows. "No. Have you had one before?"

"Nope, but I'm thinking now's as good a time as any."

"Be careful," he warned. "Tequila kicks back."

I licked some more salt and then pushed the straw aside to take bigger sips from the glass. A pleasant warm buzz spread through me from head to toe. Niiice. One more slug and I set my glass on a nearby table.

Then I glided up to Dan, wrapped one arm around his neck, and said, "Where were we?"

His gaze burned into me. "You're reckless."

I gave him a seductive smile. "What've I got to lose?"

He wrapped his arms around my waist and pulled me close. "What's this about, Trin?"

"It's about living," I whispered into his chest. "Everyone's accused me of not living, and they were right, but now I might not have that chance."

Hooking his finger under my chin, he lifted up my face. "Listen to me, you're going to be fine."

I yanked away from him and picked my

'rita back up. "You don't know that," I accused, then downed the rest in defiance. "It could all end like that," I said, attempting to snap, but failing in coordination.

Dan took my empty glass and placed it down. "Not while I'm protecting you."

I hooked my fingers through his belt loops and looked up at him. "Who are you? You don't look like a knight in shining armor."

"No?" he asked in amusement, trailing his finger down my nose. "Well, you don't look sober."

"Hey!" Miffed, I slid away from him and struck a pose. "I think I look pretty damned hot."

He grinned. "No arguments here. You look amazing."

Satisfied, I slipped into his arms. "It's your eyes."

"My eyes?" he asked, clearly not tracking our conversation.

I gave him a light smack on the back. "Pay attention. I picked this dress"—I wiggled in his embrace to remind him what dress—"because it's the color of your eyes."

"Really?" he asked, clearly pleased.

"Yeah, I couldn't forget them or *you*," I confessed, "even though I wanted to."

His thumb stroked my cheek. "I couldn't forget you, either."

I stared up into his eyes, more drunk on his nearness than on my margarita. "Dan?"

"Yeah?"

"I'm going to kiss you now."

"Please do."

I stood on my toes and pressed my lips to his. A little hesitant. A little unsure. Then I made the choice to *live* and gave in to my desire to trace his lips with the tip of my tongue. Dan sank his hands into my hair, tilting my head for better access. Something inside me unfurled, bloomed, awakened. He kissed me, breathless, and when he stopped he brushed his lips across my forehead.

"Wow," I murmured, a little bleary-eyed. "You made the world spin."

Dan's low chuckle rippled across me. "You sure that was my kiss and not the tequila?"

"Pretty sure," I sighed dreamily. "Why couldn't we meet under different circumstances?"

"I think we met the way we were supposed to."

"Through a killer?"

"No, through your dreams."

I hugged him tight. "Then maybe there's hope for us after all."

Chapter 12

"You really think this will work?" I asked.

We lay flat on our backs, fully clothed on the hotel bed, intending to take an afternoon nap.

"Makes sense, don't you think?" Dan asked, his hands folded back under his head.

I thought about it for a moment. "Yeah. There's just one problem. I can't sleep in the middle of the day."

"Sure you can," he said, looking sideways at me. "Neither one of us got any rest last night. You've got to be exhausted. Just relax."

Relax. Relax. Relax. "Not happening," I grumped and blew out a frustrated breath. Rolling on my hip, I looked at Dan. After leaving the club late last night, or rather early this morning, he'd taken me out for breakfast, plied me with coffee and aspirin, and (thankfully) intervened when I tried drunk-dialing Coral. My headache was gone but not my embarrassment. I'd come on pretty strong, but neither one of us spoke about it. And I sure didn't want to draw attention to the elephant in the room until I knew for sure how Dan felt about me.

So, for now, we pretended like nothing had happened, but we stayed hyperaware of each other.

"You gotta try, Trin," Dan coaxed. "If we sleep during the day, when he's up and about, you shouldn't have any more house calls. Then at night we can keep investigating."

"I get it." I nodded. "It's great in theory. But I can't sleep."

Dan patted his chest. I smiled and wiggled next to him, tucking my head on his shoulder. He started to twirl strands of my hair, which seemed like a good sign. Sighing deeply, I allowed the warmth and safety of his arms to soothe me. Surprising myself, I yawned.

Dan gave me a smug look.

"You feel comfy," I offered as an excuse.

"Even comfier than the bed?" he asked.

"Maybe," I answered glibly, but *definitely* is what I thought.

"Just close your eyes," he directed, still toying with my hair.

I breathed in his musky scent and relaxed. The exhaustion I'd been holding off with stubborn will pulled at me like a powerful undercurrent.

Dan chuckled softly. "I knew you could sleep."

I murmured something unintelligible.

"Sleep tight, Trin." He kissed the top of my head. "Don't let the bedbugs bite."

With those whispered words I let myself float away on the waves of sleep. I don't know how much time passed. A few hours maybe. I only know that one minute Rafe wasn't there and the next he was.

* * *

Where was I?

Darkness. Cold. Damp.

I couldn't make out much, but I smelled stagnant water and musty decay. The concrete floor was cracked and crumbly. My eyes started to adjust to the dimness, and I could tell I was in a cavernous room with exposed pipes and wooden beams. Moonlight streaked through grime-stained windows, but I still didn't know where I was. A niggling sense of familiarity tightened my tummy. Cautiously, I moved across the floor, my gaze scoping shadows. A leaking pipe's plopping pulse unnerved me. Near the end of the room I saw an office. Maybe I'd find a clue in there. Warily, I walked toward it, constantly maneuvering myself so my back was never exposed to one direction for very long.

Flap, flap, flap.

Screaming, I whirled around and saw a pigeon swooping down from the rafters. I tittered nervously and clasped my hands over

188

my chest. As I neared the office, I noticed the manager's window was actually a plate-glass two-way mirror. Only jagged shards remained in the frame, eerily reflecting back the room behind me.

Wait. Had something moved? Was someone there? I whirled around. Nothing. No one. I stepped closer to one of the full-length shards and focused on my own reflection.

Gasp!

I was wearing denim capris, a black tank top, sash belt, and beaded flip-flops. I looked down at myself. Kiri's clothes. I was wearing Kiri's clothes. That meant—

I looked back into the mirror.

Rafe.

Behind me.

He lunged and wrapped one arm around my neck in a vicious chokehold.

"Surprised, huh?" he sneered. "Did you really think you could escape me that easily?" He pulled a prescription bottle out of his pocket and shook the pills in front of my face like a

189

rattle. "I can sleep anytime. And, I can get *you* anytime."

Then he attacked.

Searing pain sliced through my body, then warm wetness and confusion.

Numb and uncomprehending, I looked into the mirror and in mute horror watched him yank a shard of broken glass from my shoulder.

"Wake up! Trinity. Wake. Up!"

Arms shook me and I heard clear urgency in a familiar voice, but I couldn't quite rise to the surface of conscious awareness.

"Oh, shit. Oh, God. What's happening?"

Dan?

He shook me again and my head flopped around like a rag doll's.

"Wake up. You have to wake up," he pleaded.

I'm trying, I wanted to tell him. *I hurt, but I'm trying.*

Then he slapped me and everything came rushing into focus. Pain, blood, fear.

I bolted upright, gasping and cupping my

right shoulder. My hand grew warm and sticky with blood.

"What the—?"

"Thank God. Oh, thank God."   •

Dan pulled me into his arms and squeezed too tight. I moaned in agony and he gently laid me back down on the bed.

"Sorry." He leaped off the bed and ran into the bathroom for towels. "For squeezing you and slapping you."

I smoothed my hand over my cheek. The sting of his slap was nothing compared to the fire in my shoulder, but it had been enough to jolt me back. "It's okay," I told him as he gently wrapped my wound in towels. "You saved me."

He yanked up the short sleeve of my tee and applied pressure to my shoulder to stop the bleeding. I gritted my teeth to keep from crying out.

"What the hell happened?"

I shook my head, still woozy and stunned. "Rafe was waiting for me. He's tweaked out on self-mutilation and sedatives."

"Sleeping pills?" Dan closed his eyes and shook his head.

"It was like he'd been expecting me."

"What happened? I heard you scream and then blood started seeping through your shirt."

"He took me to the warehouse where he killed Kiri and stabbed me with a shard of glass."

The color drained from Dan's face. "He stabbed you in your dream and it . . . it manifested itself in reality?"

"Seems so." I sat up, shaky and scared. Lifting the towel from my shoulder, I examined my wound. Rafe had stabbed me just below my collarbone. The bleeding had stopped, but I had a not-so-attractive, jagged slit.

I met Dan's stunned gaze with my own. "Man, reality bites."

Chapter 13

My Polish grandfather had a saying, "The more you sleep, the less you live."

He'd be proud. I've chosen not to sleep. *At all*.

It had been two days since I was stabbed and I was living on coffee and Vicodin. Espresso seemed to do a fair job of offsetting the meds' drowsy effect. Thankfully for me, Dan snuck home and swiped the pain pills from his mom's medicine cabinet, along with bandages and antiseptic. He patched me up as best he could without needle and thread. I wasn't about to let the guy suture me and we couldn't exactly check into the hospital without drawing a lot of attention. All in all, the shoulder wound felt okay, considering I'd been stabbed and all.

It was the sleep deprivation that was killing me.

At that moment I was trying desperately to keep myself from passing out at the Smoky Hill Library. "Sit here," Dan directed, guiding me like some fragile doll into a rolling, wood-backed chair. Obediently, I sat next to him in a small library cubicle where we had access to the Internet. The public computers were on the second floor, next to the nonfiction stacks. I'd expected the place to be dead in the evening, but it was populated with teens like me, only they were playing RuneScape and surfing MySpace.

The library would close at nine, which meant we had half an hour to figure out . . . why were we here again? I tried to see what Dan had typed into Google, but my eyes blurred and crossed.

"What . . . what're you doing?" I asked, feeling like my tongue had swelled in size.

Concern dimmed Dan's blue eyes. "Research on dreams. Remember? We talked about this."

My brain grabbed on to disconnected filaments of information. I shook my head and then felt dizzy. *"Whoooa,"* I murmured, sounding more than a little stoned. I held my head to stop the spinning.

"You okay?" Dan asked anxiously.

"Hunky-dory," I said, and then erupted into senseless giggles. "My mom says that. What does it mean?" I asked too loud.

My query was met with a terse shush by a pretty, young librarian with vibrant red hair, and an orchid tattoo. I'd noticed her earlier roving the entire area like one of those annoying Roombas. You'd think she wasn't allowed to sit or something. I placed my finger over my mouth and nodded to her that I understood. *"Shhh,"* I hissed at Dan. "You're being too loud."

He rolled his eyes as if to say, "Yeah, me," then went back to typing.

I wheeled closer and laid my head on his shoulder. "Find anything?" I whispered.

"Not yet," he answered with a smile and an eye roll.

"M'kay." Gazing up at him, I noticed he looked especially cute. In my current haze I didn't think twice about tracing the lines on his rugby shirt with my finger.

Dan turned from the webpage he'd been reading and looked directly into my eyes.

"Trin, that tickles," he said, grasping the finger I'd been tracing with to gently encourage me to stop.

"'Kay. Sorry," I said, like a giddy, overtired five-year-old. "But you look all academic and 'dorable. I can't help myself."

He chuckled. "You're pretty *a*dorable yourself."

"That's me." I yawned with a breathy gasp.

"You did that because of a lack of oxygen," Dan informed me.

I frowned. "Did what?"

"Yawned."

"Huh," I said, unimpressed. "Thought it was 'cause I'm tired."

"Well, you are. We both are."

"Mmm-hmm," I murmured.

My eyelids fluttered, my breath grew shallow, I started to drift, and—

BRUTALLY jerked myself upright and started bouncing my legs.

Dan jumped, then placed a restrictive hand on my knee. "Trin, stop. You're going to get us in trouble again."

"I can't stop!" I snapped, slapping away his hand. "I gotta stay awake."

"You're killing yourself," he said quietly, trying not to rouse any more attention from the nearby patrons who were peering over the tops of their cubbies.

"Better me kill me than him kill me," I said. "Unless you find a way to stop me from dreaming—I'm. Not. Sleeping."

Concern softened his face. "I'll find a way."

He went back to typing and I counted

books, recited the periodic table, and silently sang the words to every summer camp song I could remember. I even swiped a Smoky Hill Library pencil off the computer desk to tap the beats out on my knee, but my fingers were too uncoordinated and I kept dropping it.

"Here," Dan whispered excitedly, pointing at the screen.

I blinked and squinted but couldn't make out the text. "What's it say?"

He swiveled to face me, a relieved smile on his face. "Basically, it says we dream when we're in a R.E.M. state."

"R.E.M. I've heard of that, but—"

"Rapid Eye Movement. There are five stages of sleep. R.E.M. is the last one; it's where we dream. Our eyes move back and forth under our eyelids during that time."

"Hence the name," I said, though I still didn't get what he was so frickin' happy about. I needed more coffee. LOTS of coffee. With chocolate. Mocha. Maybe that'd make me happy. I thought I'd seen a café downstairs.

Yeah, I remembered the surprising aroma when I came in. If I could just—

"Trin!" Dan squeezed one of my hands to focus me. "Are you listening?"

I frowned and gave him a begrudging nod.

Satisfied, he said, "What it means is we *only* dream in one phase of sleep."

Yeah, 'kay? I mean, I sensed he was all excited about something and my pulse automatically revved up in response, but my poor sleep-deprived brain couldn't puzzle out what he meant. So, I shrugged.

"Don't you get it?"

Um, obviously not. Coffee might help. If I could just—

He continued as if he'd never asked me a question. "It takes two hours of sleep to reach the R.E.M. state. . . ."

I shrugged again.

Instead of getting exasperated he just laughed. Taking me by the shoulders he said, "That means if you sleep for less than two hours you won't dream."

"Say again?" I looked at him blankly. Was I having auditory hallucinations or had he said I wouldn't dream?

"You won't dream," he repeated as if he were the one hearing voices.

"Really?" I croaked, afraid to hope.

"Really," he said gently. "We could sleep in shifts."

I blinked owlishly. "I could actually sleep?"

"Yesss, Trin."

He pulled me into a hug and I let myself collapse against him.

"You can sleep," he said, rubbing my neck. "I told you I'd find a way."

I pulled back and rested my forehead against his. "And he won't be able to get me?" I asked fearfully.

"He won't," Dan assured me, kissing the tip of my nose. "Not as long as we wake you before the two-hour mark."

I sat still and silent for a long moment. A wash of numbness went through me. Hope, fear, hope, fear. Hope! "So, I can take a nap and I'll be safe?" I whispered.

"Yeah." He caressed my cheek. "Does a nap sound good?"

He got his answer when I grabbed his face in my hands, kissed his lips, and promptly burst into tears.

Chapter 14

"*N*ow I lay me down to sleep," I whispered, as I startled myself awake once more. "I pray the Lord my soul to keep. If I should die before I wake—"

"Stop that," Dan ordered. "This'll work. I promise."

I didn't know what to believe.

It had been forty-eight hours since I'd slept.

Four days since I'd made a deal with Robert Devlin's son.

Five days since I'd started playing cat and mouse with crazed, supernatural killer Rafe Stevens.

Almost a week since he'd entered my dreams.

And just over a year since he'd committed his first murder.

My life had become a waking and sleeping nightmare.

You know that old wives' tale that says if you die in your dreams you'll die for real?

I never believed it.

Now I do.

My head on his lap, I peered up at Dan. It was a little after midnight and my emotions were raw and ragged from lack of sleep. I had to completely rely on him, for better or worse.

"He can't get you," Dan swore. "Please. Trust me."

Trust had been a tenuous thing between us, but I'd asked him to have faith in me. Now I had to do the same.

Looking into his blue eyes, I took a leap of faith and jumped into the abyss.

Since I hadn't slept for forty-eight hours, you'd think a two-hour nap would seem like a cruel tease. That I'd wake up groggy and bitchy, begging for more Zs.

Instead, when Dan gently shook me awake, I found myself coming to with a huge smile on my face.

Hallelujah! I'd lived to sleep another day.

Don't get me wrong, I still felt tired, but I was alive. *Alive!* And I'd had zip, zero, zilch dreams. No Rafe. No anyone.

Relief positively energized me.

When Dan settled down to sleep, I was all too happy to play timekeeper. I seriously can't say how stoked I felt to have caught a few dreamless winks. It gave me hope we could beat Rafe. With the entire state on the hunt, and me able to stay out of dream's reach, our chances of survival had monumentally increased.

So, while Dan slept I attempted to occupy myself. I sat next to him, flipping through magazines and channel surfing, but watching him seemed to be the only thing I could do with any true focus.

His dark hair stood up in these cute little tufts, and his full lips made me yearn for more of his kisses. But for now I was content to watch the rise and fall of his chest and lightly run my fingers over the stubble on his cheeks. Five o'clock shadow was so sexy and Dan made it look good.

I even liked the rumbly way he softly snored. The poor guy hadn't slept much in the last two days. Not because he couldn't, but because he'd been worried about me and had kept me company through my sleeplessness. He'd only allowed himself three or four hours of rest.

Now it was my turn to take care of him.

The clock would sound in one minute, but I wanted to give him more than two hours so I disengaged the alarm and went into the bathroom to fix a fresh pot of coffee. Swanky hotel that this was, we had gourmet ground coffee in those mess-free, pre-filled filters. I poured water into the chamber, plunked a pouch into the basket, turned it on, and— *voilá*—burble, burble, brew. I poured myself a cup and sat in a leather upholstered chair. Intent on staying awake, I inhaled the yummy, strong scent.

I took a sip and gave an appreciative sigh. Even "bad" coffee deserved a moment of worship and this was five-star coffee.

Dan gave a low moan in his sleep. Hmm. Maybe the bikinis were back. I smiled and took another hit of my java. Then he huffed out a breath, like the wind had been knocked out of him. Weird. I walked over to his side of the bed.

"Dan?" I whispered.

Nothing.

He lay still and quiet. I watched him closely, peering over the lip of my mug. His eyes were moving back and forth under his lids. He'd definitely hit R.E.M. I was just about to settle back in my chair when he doubled up as if he'd been hit in the stomach. I gasped and set my mug on the nightstand. Lifting his shirt I saw a welt where his stomach had been punched.

Rafe.

"No!" I cried.

Stone-cold terror assaulted me. This could

not be happening. Rafe had never harmed anyone but me. I couldn't live with myself if he hurt Dan.

"Wake up!" I shook him. "Come on, Dan," I begged.

His head snapped to the left as if someone had delivered a right cross. A small cut split open his cheekbone — but his eyelids still moved with the signs of R.E.M.

"Stop it!" My wasted screams were meant for Rafe. "Please," I pleaded, as I shook Dan's body, "please wake up before it's too late." Then I remembered the slap Dan had used to wake me up. *Smack!* But, despite the red palm print I left on his cheek, Dan didn't respond. Desperate, I looked around the room and my gaze fell on my mug. I grabbed the hot coffee and hesitated, not wanting to hurt him. *Better a slight burn than* . . . Heart in my throat, I flung the contents at Dan's chest. He hollered and then opened his eyes.

"Oh my God. Oh my God," I chanted. Tossing the mug to the floor, I scrambled onto the bed and grabbed the hem of his sopping shirt, carefully working it up and over his head. "Are you okay?"

"Holy shit," Dan stuttered. "He got me. *Me!*"

"I couldn't wake you. I tried and tried. The coffee was the only thing I could think of," I babbled.

"It worked," Dan croaked. His chest looked red and angry but unblistered. Signs of the damage Rafe had done slowly ripened across his skin like a developing Polaroid of bruises. "If you hadn't—"

"I can't believe this," I interrupted. "I let you sleep longer because you've taken such good care of me and . . ."

Dan grabbed his head with both hands and squeezed his eyes shut. "That monster was in my frickin' head!" He looked at me, stricken, and said, "I don't know how you deal with that, Trin. I feel—"

"Violated?" I asked tearfully.

"Yeah," he murmured. "And to think I've been pushing you . . ."

I wrapped my arms around his neck in a gentle hug. "I was so scared. If I'd lost you . . ."

He pulled me toward him. "You didn't."

"Why did he attack you?" I asked, pushing away just far enough to look into his eyes.

Dan hesitated, then said, "Because he couldn't get you."

I burst into tears—such a stupid girly thing to do, I know—all my earlier hopes were crushed. What had I done to deserve this? I'd always strived to be invisible, to seep into my surroundings rather than stand out, and now I'd been singled out in the worst imaginable way. Dan had been hurt because of me. When I thought I might lose him . . .

Suddenly, anger crackled through me. How dare Rafe come after Dan? He had nothing to do with this. This was between me, Rafe, and Kiri.

I had to find a way to stop him.

I swiped away my tears with my fists and got Dan a damp towel.

"That's going to look ugly tomorrow," I told

him as I washed the cut on his cheek.

"It'll make me look tough, though," he said, wincing.

"I'm hoping you look worse than you feel."

"That bad, huh?" he said wryly.

"Not really," I assured him with a smile. "I just hate that you're hurt because of me."

"It's not *because* of you," he said in a grim voice. "It's because of Rafe. You got me out of there just in time." He clutched his head again, still feeling the effects of Rafe's attack. "Neither one of us imagined he'd come after me."

"I should've—"

"Trinity, quit beating yourself up. I'm beaten enough for the two of us."

I leaned in then and impulsively brushed his cheekbone with a gentle kiss. "Does that feel better?" I asked, pulling away.

His eyes darkened. "Much."

I smiled and laid a kiss on his pinkened chest. "And that?"

"Definitely."

I angled closer, my breath mingling with his, and very slowly pressed my lips to his. "And this?"

"*Mmm*, good," he answered quietly.

His arms wrapped around me and pulled me close. Adrenaline rushed through me. I didn't know if residual fear from the attack drove me or if I simply wanted to give in to my attraction. Either way, I took his mouth in a hungry kiss. He groaned as I accidentally grazed his cut lip and I pulled away.

He shook his head. "Don't stop."

I cupped his face in my hands. "I don't want to hurt you."

"You couldn't possibly hurt me with a kiss."

I peppered little kisses on his battered face. He responded by rolling me to my back and gazing down at me.

"This is crazy," I whispered. "All of this."

"It is," Dan agreed, stroking my cheek. "But right now you're all that makes sense to me."

Hooking one hand around Dan's neck, I

drew him down for more kisses. He pressed me against the bed and nibbled the side of my neck, making me shiver.

"Do you want to?" he asked in a ragged breath.

Did I? Ordinarily, a girl in my sitch ought to be scared and full of second thoughts, but we had been living a nightmare for days and I was ready for a little wide-awake fantasy.

I knew that by morning I might have regrets.

But sometimes the morning doesn't come.

"Why didn't you tell me you'd never—?"

My head on Dan's shoulder, I absently twirled a lock of my hair. "I didn't want to sound like one of those movies," I said wistfully. "You know those dramatic 'I-don't-want-to-die-a-virgin' scenes?"

He laughed. "Is that why you wanted to?"

"No. Yes. Partly."

"Well, I'm glad that's clear."

I looked into his eyes. "I wanted to feel alive. With *you*."

He stroked his hand down my arm and clasped my hand. "And did you?"

"Oh, yeah," I told him with a soft smile. "You're good for me."

"Really," he said. "How's that?"

"Well, there's the obvious," I said, rubbing my leg against his. "That was definitely good. And then there's the fact that you may have just gotten me an A on my homework assignment."

"Huh."

I giggled. "Coral gave me an assignment for the summer, and I believe you"—I kissed his chest—"just helped me pass with flying colors."

"There you go using me again," he said with mock outrage. "But I guess if this is the kind of homework you have to do, then maybe I can help out."

"You are so generous."

He tickled my ribs. "So when's your next assignment due?"

Laughing, I tried to push him away. "Wait, I think you're getting the wrong idea here."

"No, no," he said. "I'm pretty sure I have the right idea."

Then he kissed me and I realized something. Not only had I finally started living, I'd started loving, too.

Chapter 15

The phrase "I lost my virginity" kept rolling through my head like a scrolling LED sign. Ridiculously, I wondered if I looked different.

I felt different.

Somehow more and less. I'd forever given a part of myself away, but at the same time I'd gained a new understanding of myself.

And I didn't second-guess things, at all. What was the sense in wondering if I'd done the right thing, with the right guy, at the right time? There's no time like the present when death stalks you.

Life can be hysterically ironic.

If you had told me five days ago that I'd fall for the devil's son, I would've gone medieval on your ass. And yet here I was . . .

I brushed my lips across Dan's bare back and snuck out of bed. In the bathroom I studied my reflection and found I looked exactly the same, except for a happy, knowing sparkle in my eye.

"Trin," Dan called. "Trin?"

I stepped out of the bathroom and almost walked into Dan's chest.

"There you are," he said, looking a little embarrassed. "I thought maybe you'd . . ."

"I'd what?"

He didn't say anything.

"You didn't think I left, did you?"

"I didn't know." He shrugged. "Morning after and all . . ."

I wrapped my arms around my waist. "I don't scare off that easily."

"No," he said and brushed my lips with his. "I should know that about you by now."

We kept kissing until Dan's cell phone rang.

While he answered it, I went into the bathroom to make coffee and caught snatches of his conversation.

"I really don't see how that's any of your business," he said tersely.

Was he talking to Kelley? I stiffened.

"Yeah," Dan sniped, "she's with me and we're both fine."

His dad. The tone of his voice definitely said it was his dad. Why would Mr. Devlin be asking about *me*?

"You need to find him," Dan ordered. "We've hit dead ends everywhere."

After fixing coffee, I straightened the bathroom. All I wanted to do was hide from the discomfort created by their animosity. Once again I felt like I was intruding on something really private between Dan and his dad.

"What?!" Dan gasped.

The hair on my neck stood up.

"Are you okay?" he asked, his tone veering from his usual aggravation to uncharacteristic concern.

I stepped closer to the bathroom door. The shift in Dan's voice was alarming. Something terrible must've happened.

"You're sure? He said that?

217

"No, I can't come home. Not until Trinity's safe.

"Dad, listen. You have to sleep in two-hour shifts. Then you won't dream. Don't let the nursing staff sedate you."

Dad? Dream? Nurses? Surely Rafe hadn't . . . I stepped out of the bathroom and looked at Dan. He sat on the edge of the bed, fear darkening his eyes.

"If you mean that," he said, his voice young and vulnerable, "you can change.

"Yes, you can," he said, his tone stern. "But if something happens to me—no, let me finish— if something happens I want you to promise you'll do what you said. Be a better man.

"I—I'm glad you called. I will."

Dan looked me in the eyes, and I saw how much his dad had hurt him. Just now some of that had been mended.

"We'll stay safe," he promised, his voice thick with emotion. "'Bye."

I gave him a moment to compose himself and then sat next to him. "Rafe?"

"Yeah." Dan scrubbed his face with his

hands. "He attacked my dad last night after you woke me. He's in the hospital with a broken nose, three busted ribs, and a concussion."

"My God," I gasped.

"Mom couldn't wake him. The only reason he survived is because Rafe didn't want to kill him."

"How's he doing?"

"They're both wigging out."

"Being attacked in your dreams can do that to a person."

"He . . ." Dan closed his eyes for a moment and ran his hand over his mouth. "My dad actually apologized. Said he had no idea what he would unleash when he helped Rafe."

"He admitted it?" I asked, more than a little stunned.

"I know, I can't believe it," he said, shaking his head. "Never in my life did I expect him to cop to that, let alone say I'm sorry. He told me about Erskine. Everything. I'm just stunned." He took my hand in his and I felt tiny trembles in his fingers. "Guess a near-death experience can give you a whole new perspective."

"Guess so," I said. But I couldn't help wondering just how "changed" Mr. Devlin was. Don't get me wrong, I was happy he'd confessed and apologized, but he owed Dan far more than that.

"He's looking for Rafe," Dan continued, "but he's hit the same walls we have." He paused and gave me a concerned look. "Trinity, I'm not sure Rafe can be found."

"He's got to slip up sometime," I argued. "He has to eat. Go out. Refill his meds."

"Maybe," Dan said. "But think." He gave me a grave look that caused prickles up and down my arms. "We're applying human logic to a man who defies it. Who knows what he's capable of?"

"You're right. Rules don't apply to him." An edge of hysteria tinged my voice as I realized we might not survive Rafe.

"I don't want to scare you even more, Trin, but he's playing for keeps." Dan took my other hand in his. "He left you a message."

A wash of dizziness came over me. "What?"

Dan swallowed hard, clearly reluctant to tell me.

"He wants you—"

Dan rubbed my fingers in a nervous gesture.

"Rafe said you should give yourself up," he continued, "or he'll go through everyone you love, one by one, until you do."

I went numb and the sharp taste of acid burned the back of my throat. Then panic constricted my chest. The world stopped. Buzzing panic deafened the noise around me and my extremities went lax.

"*Moooom!*"

My entire life I'd disdained and denied my gift.

Now it might be the only thing that could save me and those I loved.

Getting hold of my mom made me so weak with relief, I nearly passed out. I thought about coming clean with her, but I knew if I told her I was in deep doo-doo she'd be on the first plane back, despite the danger that would put her in.

She was due home on Friday, two days from now. I feared never seeing her again, but despite the rock-sized lump in my throat I managed to keep a level tone as I said good-bye. As soon as I hung up I came unglued. We're talking snotty, chest-quaking sobs. I just prayed she stayed safe and I stayed alive long enough to see all the kitschy tourist crap she brought home.

Rafe hadn't visited her. Thank God! I think she was too far away. The power that kind of dream walking would entail went beyond even his capabilities. For the moment.

And luckily, Rafe didn't know a thing about Coral. In fact, I'd gotten a text from her that morning begging for more deets on Dan and saying she wanted to meet him on Saturday when she got back. She was safe for the time being.

But I had this sick feeling that Rafe's abilities were growing and strengthening at a rapid rate. I had to stop him before he became invincible.

I'd never willingly explored or opened myself up to my ability. For me, it always meant pain and darkness. But here, now, I saw what real darkness looked like. To stop its spread, I needed to embrace my talent and use it against Rafe in the same way he'd used his powers against me.

It was time to fight.

I prayed I was ready. But first I had to ask for Dan's help.

I'd left him on the beach later that afternoon and told him I needed to clear my head. I think he needed to do the same. We'd spent a quiet day together, going out to eat, shopping, and walking along the shore. Neither of us talked much. We were content in each other's company and lost in our own thoughts.

Evening came fast. Too fast.

I found Dan sitting with his toes buried in the sand, head raised, contemplating the clouds. Reluctantly, I stepped into his line of vision.

"Hi," I said, twisting my fingers in nervous agitation.

"Hi," he said back, patting the sand between his legs.

I sat and he wrapped his arms around me. I rested my head on his shoulder and allowed myself to enjoy the moment. His musky scent, mixed with the salty ocean breeze, made me smile. It felt right to be in his arms and not just because we were caught up in a life-or-death drama. It felt right because it was.

"Trinity, I—"

"I've got a plan," I interrupted.

He looked down at me. "For what?"

"You were right. We may never find Rafe and now a lot of people are in danger. Not just me."

"And you're thinking?"

I sat quietly for a moment and wrapped his arms tighter around me. Why couldn't I be a normal girl, with a normal boyfriend, spending some normal romantic time on the beach?

Dan shrugged to nudge me into answering.

I sighed and tilted my head back to look at him. "I'm thinking it's time to fight back."

Step-by-step, I outlined my plan to him. His eyes widened a few times and the line of his mouth grew thinner.

224

"It's risky," I finished. "There's no saying either one of us will come out alive."

He rested his forehead against mine. "A fighting chance is better than no chance. But are you sure about my part in this?"

"Yes," I encouraged him. "Anyone can have a lucid dream. You just have to want to."

He shook his head. "I can't imagine it's that easy."

"No," I agreed, "but I'll be there to pull you through. Don't worry."

He tucked a piece of hair around my ear. "It's not me I'm worried about. I don't want to get into the—what did you call it?"

"Dreamscape."

"Right. What if I'm in the dreamscape and then I can't help you because I'm having some stupid spring-break dream?"

I smiled. "Just focus on what you want to dream about before you go to sleep. Focus on me."

"That part's easy," he said. "About last night, I—"

"Please don't say it," I blurted, spinning

around to face him. "Don't say you regret sleeping with me."

He yanked me into his arms and shut me up with his mouth. One of his hands slid into my hair and the other one caressed my cheek. He kissed away my fear of rejection, then he pulled back and said, "Trin, I wasn't going to say that. I have no regrets. How could I?"

"I don't know. I just got scared for a sec."

"You don't regret—"

"No!" I insisted.

"Then we'll see this through together and, when we do, I want to take you on a real date," he offered. "That's what I wanted to say. A real date should've come first."

"Date?" I choked. That's what he'd wanted to tell me? At a time like this? I almost laughed, but relief made my insides bubble like champagne.

He kissed the tip of my nose. "Yep, a date. In case you didn't realize it, our relationship has been a little, er, unconventional."

I placed a kiss on his chin. "I'd like that," I said wistfully.

"Good."

He stood and pulled me up into his arms. I liked the way we fit. The way the top of my head tucked right beneath his chin. When Dan placed a tender kiss on my forehead I realized there was something stronger than my abilities between us.

"Ready?" he asked.

"Yeah," I said, armed with something I hadn't had before. "Let's go kick Rafe's ass."

Chapter 16

*H*ere I was being all alpha bitch, ready for an ass-kicking, dream-world showdown, yet I couldn't say three little words to Dan beforehand. My entire life I'd let my gift separate me from everyone. I purposely didn't build friendships, let alone romantic relationships, because of it. As much as I was changing, grabbing on to life, I couldn't completely break free of my old habits. Besides, a part of me was scared I'd seal our fate if I said those words. I didn't want this love story to end all *Romeo and Juliet*.

As Dan and I settled onto the bed, my heart hammered painfully in my chest. My plan wasn't foolproof. All I could do was listen to my instincts. I could beat Rafe at his own game if I trusted my own abilities. If I trusted Dan. If I *believed*.

Now came the terrifying reality.

But Rafe had nothing on me. I was the original dream walker. I'd been doing this longer than he had. I finally understood what it meant to really live. And I refused to give that up.

Instead, I planned to make Rafe wish he'd never gone to sleep.

"Let's do this," I said.

"That's my girl," Dan said. Using one of his tube socks, he lashed our wrists together. "Too tight?"

I gave an experimental tug. "No." I clasped his hand in mine. "I might even like it," I offered.

Dan gave me a sexy wink. "Remind me of that later."

Holding hands, we lay on the bed, my head propped on his shoulder. "Let's go over it one last time," I suggested. "Once you start snoring—"

"I do *not* snore," he said in mock outrage.

"Whatever." I rolled my eyes. "Once you start, um, breathing loudly," I continued, "I'll let myself fall asleep so I can follow you."

"Then two hours later," he added, "we'll hit the R.E.M. stage—"

"And Rafe," I finished.

"Yeah. And if we're lucky," Dan said, "you'll enter my dreamscape just a few minutes behind me."

I hoped it wouldn't take me more than a couple of minutes to doze off after Dan. Then, because we were tied together and couldn't roll apart, I'd enter his dream, just as I had on bikini beach.

"Remember," I told him, "tell yourself you're in charge of your dream, you're aware of your surroundings, you're mentally present."

"And I'll concentrate on you."

"Dan . . ." I hesitated, "whatever happens, I want you to know you've changed my life."

"Are we back to that homework assignment?" he teased.

"No, I'm serious." I looked him in the eyes.

"You've showed me what it is to live. To really be *me*."

"Good," he encouraged me. "When we're done, you can introduce that great girl to the rest of the world."

I kissed him. "See you on the other side," I whispered, then held him tightly, probably too tightly, as I waited for his breathing to even out. Time seemed to slow down and stretch out like a barren highway until Dan finally started to snore.

Told you.

I raised myself on one shoulder and took a good look at his face. "I'm on my way." Despite the fear clutching my chest, I settled into his arms and let myself drift off to find him. As I floated into slumber I remembered something James Dean once said: "Dream as if you'll live forever, live as if you'll die today."

There was one risk with our plan I'd refused to consider. Dan had voiced his concern, but I stupidly dismissed his worry.

I shouldn't have.

I popped into Dan's dream as planned, but he wasn't lucid. This was just an ordinary dream as far as he was concerned. That didn't bode well for either of us.

Especially when Rafe showed up.

We sat at a small parlor table in Dan's kitchen before a breakfast of steak and eggs. Dan chatted about innocuous things, and I tried desperately to snap him into awareness. Since I didn't play to character, Dan looked at me like I'd grown two heads.

"Why do you keep telling me to 'focus'?" he asked with more than a little aggravation. "I'm fine. You're the one not making any sense."

I felt like banging my head on the table, but then I heard the front door open and I tensed.

Rafe walked into the room with a malicious grin. "Honey, I'm home," he said, sounding like Jack Nicholson in *The Shining*.

"Great," Dan muttered to me under his breath. "Dad, what're you doing here?" he asked, sounding anything but welcoming.

Dad?

Oh, this was bad. Really bad.

I had to stay in character so that Rafe wouldn't suspect I was more than just an actor in Dan's dream. "Hi, Mr. Devlin."

He ignored me and honed in on Dan. Realizing Dan saw him as his father obviously appealed to every sadistic bone in Rafe's body.

"How's it hanging, Sonny Boy?" he asked, giving Dan a too-hard slap on the back. "Have I got plans for you."

"Trinity and I already have plans," Dan said evenly.

"Cancel them," Rafe ordered. Turning his malignant gaze on me, he said, "She won't be around much longer."

A bone-deep shiver ran through me, but I tried to act naturally.

"You can't kick her out," Dan argued. "She's my girlfriend. If she goes, I go."

Rafe shrugged. "Works for me."

Dan fisted his hands on the table. He couldn't get into a fight with Rafe because he'd get hurt. Dan didn't have a sentient presence to give power to his actions. Rafe did.

"It's okay," I whispered, hoping to soothe his growing anger. At this point I didn't know what to do. I had to find a way out of this dream. I couldn't take Rafe on alone.

"'It's okay,'" Rafe mimicked. "I should've known you don't wear the pants in your relationship, Junior."

Dan slapped the table. "That's enough."

Rafe raised an eyebrow. I could see how much he enjoyed taunting Dan. I didn't want this to get physical.

"Come on, babe," I told Dan, rising from my chair. "Let's get out of here."

Where we'd go, I didn't know. But surely if we walked out the front door—

"You're not going anywhere," Rafe said, placing a heavy hand on Dan's shoulder.

"What do you want from me?" Dan spat.

"I want to tell you what a sniveling, coward, no-good son you are."

Dan flinched and his gaze flicked to mine, before lowering.

"Did you hear me?" Rafe barked. "You're nothing!"

"Leave him alone! Mr. Devlin," I added hastily, playing along. Then I sat down and toyed with my fork.

Rafe's baleful glare took me in and I witnessed the exact moment that he decided to change his tactics. A malicious smirk twisted his face.

"You've got more guts than my boy does," he started.

Rafe ambled around the table to stand behind me. He stroked my ponytail and it took everything in me not to gag.

"What're you doing with a freak like her?" he asked Dan. "She couldn't even save that little girl."

"Get away from her," Dan growled.

Rafe's loathsome laugh crept up my spine like the legs of a spider. "I don't think so." He wrapped my ponytail around his fist and yanked my head back. Looking Dan directly in the eye, he asked, "How 'bout I just get rid of her?"

Dan shot out of his chair and moved to grab Rafe, but his hands passed through him.

Rafe shoved my head forward and stood to face a bewildered Dan.

"Sucks to be you," Rafe said. "You can't touch me, but I can touch you."

And there was the problem. In the dreamiverse, a non-sentient can't touch a lucid dreamer, but the lucid dreamer can make contact with the non-sentient.

With those uneven odds, Rafe delivered a right cross to Dan's jaw and a sickening, bone-crunching blow to his nose. Dan flew back, hitting the floor with a thud. Blood gushed out of his nostrils.

"No!" I screamed, rushing to Dan's side. This wasn't the way things were supposed to go. Trembling, I ran my fingers over Dan's face. I knew in reality, where we lay in our bed, Dan had a broken nose and two blackening eyes. What seemed real here would be even worse in the waking world. I grabbed a kitchen towel and pressed it to Dan's nose to stem the bleeding.

The white cotton quickly bloomed red. What had I been thinking dragging him into this?

He was defenseless!

Rafe would kill him.

It would be my fault.

And all the while he'd believe his attacker was his own father.

If we were going to have a fighting chance, I *had* to find a way to make him lucid.

"Come on, Dan," I pleaded. "Don't give up. I need you here. *All* of you."

"Get out, Trin," he answered, his voice ragged with pain. "I don't want my dad to hurt you, too."

Dan didn't get it. I had to do something to yank him into awareness. If Rafe was paying attention he'd see I'd broken the dreamiverse rules by touching Dan. But it was now or never.

"Go," Dan said. "Before my dad—"

"No!" I shouted, trusting my gut.

There was no way out.

I had to do this.

"Dan, that's not your dad. Look!" I pointed.

"*Really* look. That's Rafe."

"Well, I'll be damned," Rafe drawled. "Looks like I'm not the only one sleeping with Dan."

Now I was in it.

Rafe knew he had me right where he wanted me.

"Rafe?" Dan asked, sounding puzzled. He looked at the man he thought was his father. "What the—how'd he get here?"

"You see him?" I asked excitedly.

"Yeah, let's get out of here." He tried to grab my hand but couldn't connect.

In horror I realized that Dan saw Rafe because I told him to, not because he had conscious awareness.

Rafe moseyed closer, a manic gleam in eyes. "Girly, you and me got some catching up to do," he said.

This was it. The end. Game over.

Tears running down my face, I kissed Dan's cheek and said the three words I've been unable to voice in the real world. "I love you."

"Aw, isn't that sweet," Rafe said in a caustic voice. He hauled me off the floor by my arms and pressed his nose against mine. "Too bad you aren't going to live to enjoy it."

Anger and resentment welled up inside me. I was going to *live*, damn it! In self-defense, I shoved against Rafe's chest, putting all the force of my emotion behind it. To my surprise, he flew back and hit the wall.

Whoa!

If ever there was a time to open myself up to my gift, to see what I was made of, now was it. Mentally I opened my heart and mind. Like a long corridor in a hotel, doors flung open on both sides, power emerging from the once-blocked portals. Strength surged through me. I could see that Rafe felt the shift in power, too. He pulled out a razor and nicked a tic-tac-toe grid on his arm. Blood ran, and Rafe drew himself up straighter, high on the rush of pain.

I laughed to cover my worry. "You empower yourself on blood and pain. My strength comes from love and acceptance. Which of the two do you think is stronger?" I asked.

Dan still sat on the floor. He held his head

between his hands. "Trin?" he asked, sounding confused.

"It's all right," I assured him. "It's just a bad dream."

"You can say *that* again," Rafe sneered. "Kind of like the one you had about Kiri. Too bad you didn't get to her in time."

Mentally I flinched, but physically I refused to show he'd hit a nerve.

Two could play at this game. Pulling on my new forces, I tried to change the dreamscape. It required immense mental concentration, a kind I'd never used before, but after a couple tries I magically altered our setting.

Miami State Prison.

Rafe stood in a cell. I stood just outside it. Dan sat on the floor next to me, looking baffled. The stark walls blurred for a moment, but I mentally braced the imagery so it snapped into full focus.

"Seem familiar?" I asked Rafe. "It's where you belong."

He paled. The blood on his arm congealed, and with it, his pain and power diminished.

"You're not crazy, just sick and evil," I told him. "You should fit in perfectly here."

Rafe grabbed the bars and tried to yank them open, but they were secure.

"You took a child's life and you've toyed with so many others. I'll see that you end up here," I swore with vehemence.

Dan stood. "How'd we get here? Am I awake or asleep?"

In quick succession Rafe sliced a ladder of marks down the inside of both his arms, but panic made him careless and he sliced an artery. Blood pumped out with every beat of his heart. He roared, and Dan and I took a step back. It didn't sound like a shout of pain so much as the kind of thing Milt had described, an amping up of power.

"I've only begun to toy with you," he threatened. "This comes to an end. Now."

He squeezed the cuts on his arms and shut his eyes in fierce concentration.

He was trying to change the dreamscape!

I willed it to stay the same. My head hurt with the effort. I felt my focus slipping, my energy diminishing. Rafe continued to dig at the cuts on his arm and my dreamscape dissolved and reappeared as something new.

We stood on a rocky cliff high above a beach, an impossibility in flat Miami. Rafe had created this dangerous precipice from his own imagination and added special effects for drama. Rain lashed down in sheets and lightning flashed. Dan stood at my back; both of us had our shoulders pressed tight to the rock wall behind us. Only five feet stood between our shoes and the cliff's edge. Rafe faced me, a look of maniacal determination in his eyes. Immediately, I understood the implications of the setting he'd chosen. It would be him or me—over the edge.

Terror gripped me as I looked over the crumbly cliffside to the violent, choppy waters a hundred feet below. I tried to remind myself that, in reality, Rafe lay in a bed somewhere, slowly bleeding to death. Suddenly, the dreamscape started to fade. The stormy beach setting took a lot of power for Rafe to maintain. In desperation he sliced one of his wrists again. The pounding rain mixed with his blood and ran in rivulets down his fingers to the sodden ground.

"You're killing yourself!" I shouted. While I wanted this lunatic out of my life, I couldn't stand to watch him commit suicide.

"Never!" he yelled, but then his image began to flicker and vibrate like an old movie reel. To keep himself present he massaged his wrists to elicit pain. Again three-dimensional, he lunged for me.

Arms entwined, we grappled on the small edge. Twice my left foot slipped off the side, sending wet gravel tumbling down. I desperately wanted to change the dreamscape, but I had to keep my entire focus on Rafe in order to survive this confrontation. Just as I felt my muscles weaken and my body lean sideways, too close to the rim, Dan shouted, "Let her go!" Then he grabbed me by the waist and yanked me back toward the wall. Pulled off balance, Rafe stumbled and let go of me. He crashed into the rock wall headfirst.

Dan was here. Really here. I gave him a

brief hug, never taking my eyes off Rafe. "You made it!" I said.

Dan squeezed me back. "I started to 'come to' in the jail. A little confused but—"

Rafe turned around, a bloody gash on his forehead. He looked like something out of a horror movie. Red streaks ran down his face, a mixture of blood and rain. His arms and hands were just as gory and his clothes were stained. His eyes almost looked otherworldly, the way they gleamed with madness.

"He's getting weak from blood loss and using so much power to maintain this"—I motioned to our surroundings—"maybe if we stall—"

Rafe had other plans.

"Come to play?" he asked Dan with a sneer. "Took you long enough."

"Better late than never," Dan retorted.

Rafe leaped forward and threw a punch, which Dan blocked. "Sucks to be you," he said, echoing Rafe's earlier taunt.

"Don't hit him," I yelled at Dan. "It'll just make him stronger."

I'm sure it took every ounce of self-control for Dan not to pound Rafe in retaliation. Instead he shoved him away.

But Rafe wanted — no, needed — to instigate a fight with Dan. He rushed him like a linebacker. At the last second, Dan ducked low under Rafe's stomach and then stood up, flipping him over his shoulders. Rafe landed hard on his back, winded.

Assessing the situation, I tried to find a way to work things to my advantage. I didn't want to change the dreamscape, because I knew controlling it weakened Rafe, but maybe I could enhance it. Using my power, I created a low-lying, thick fog, which hid the cliff's edge.

When Rafe stood his feet weren't visible.

"Rafe," I said, "you dropped something." Then I tossed the razor blade that had fallen out of his pocket. The pitch went a little high and to the right. Instinctually, Rafe stepped back to catch it. His hand caught the blade, but his feet had found the invisible edge. He tottered and windmilled his arms for balance, but like a slo-mo shot in a movie he slipped off the brink, a wide-eyed look of terror on his face.

His scream echoed as he plummeted down a deadly drop.

Dan and I jolted awake, gasping in shock.

It was over.

Chapter 17

"So, after this summer, what would your coming-of-age novel be called?" I asked Coral.

We were back at SoBe, except this time I was wearing an adorable white, retro dress with black polka dots and red scallop trim. Not to mention my killer 1940s red, peep-toe sling-back heels. Granted, they were sitting underneath my lounge chair, but they still made the outfit.

The occasion?

A good-bye party for me and Coral.

"*Hmm.* Title?" She tapped her finger against her lips. "Probably *The Freckles and Foibles of GingerChick.*"

I laughed. "That is *so* you."

"Natch," she said, fluffing her red hair. "And a total best seller."

"Of course."

"And yours?"

I didn't even have to think about it. *"In Your Dreams,"* I said with a grin.

"Brilliantly apropos," Coral said with applause. "It's a little bit of a warning, and a little bit of a kiss-off—and it says that you've accepted your ability."

"Yep," I agreed with a smug nod. "It says it all."

Shaking her head, Coral added, "I still can't believe everything you went through while I was gone. My story's all chicklit light and yours is a woman-in-jeopardy thriller."

I held up a finger. "Don't forget the romance."

"Overachiever," she accused. "I told you to go out and live. I didn't mean you should stare death in the face first."

I cracked up. "Yes, well, some extreme make-overs require extreme measures."

"God, it's so good to see you happy." Her eyes brightened with tears. "To finally know *everything* about you."

Smiling, I reached for her hand. All I could say was, "I'm sorry I didn't tell you sooner."

She gave my hand a squeeze and then dabbed at her eyes. "I understand why you were afraid, but nothing you could do would scare me off. You"—she pointed at me—"are my partner in crime."

"Your sidekick."

"My dream warrior."

"Your wingwoman."

"That's right!" She sat up a little straighter. "Now *you* can help *me* find a guy."

"Have pants, will travel," I said with exaggerated seriousness and we both started giggling. Then in all earnestness I asked, "You think we're ready?"

"Abso—tootin'—lutely," she said and smacked me a high five, "but UM may not be ready for *us*."

"You can say that again," my mom said

with a smile, then scootched my legs and sat down on the end of my chair. "Enjoying your-selves?"

"It's great, Mom." I waved my hand to encompass all the food, the presents, the bal-loons, and the perfect beach setting. "Exactly the send-off we wanted."

"I can't believe it's time," she said wistfully, tucking a strand of hair behind my ear.

I gave her the same reassuring smile I'd given her that morning when she'd said the same thing. And yesterday. And the day before. "Classes start in four days."

"Are you sure you don't want me to drive up with you today?" she offered.

"I'm sure," I insisted. "Dan will take good care of me."

"I know," she said. "He already has."

"Cheer up, Raina," Coral said. "At least she's not going off to school *and* dating pond scum."

"There is *that*," she agreed with a half-hearted laugh, then shook her head. "It's just . . . I leave for eight days, *eight days*, and everything changes."

I wrapped my arms around my mom. "I think it was meant to happen."

"You're probably right"—she held me tight—"but still . . ."

She and Coral had been home for about a week and in that time I'd filled them in on everything. Yes, even *that*. There were no more secrets. No more holding back. No more fear. Coral told me I had indeed received an A on my homework, but my mom had beaten herself up for leaving me alone. And she was furious with me for not calling her when Rafe escaped. In the end she was thrilled that 1) I was safe, 2) I had finally embraced my gift, 3) I'd taken her advice and started *living*, 4) I'd told Coral everything, and 5) I'd found a great boyfriend. But she was now afraid to let me out of her sight, which made my departure for UM particularly difficult.

I pulled out of her embrace. "Mom, you can come up and see me next weekend," I reminded her. "Coral and I will have everything set up in our room by then."

"You can compliment our sense of style," Coral suggested. "And take us out to eat."

Mom didn't smile. "I'll do that, but—"

"Rafe's gone," I said quietly. "For good."

She sighed. "I keep reading the newspaper clippings to remind myself of that."

Suicide. That's what the papers called it. The police had found Rafe's body, sliced to ribbons, in a seedy hotel. Everyone had been shocked that he'd escaped, only to kill himself.

I knew better.

I also knew it was time for me to heal. To move on. To fly free and live.

I nudged my mom. "Remember *your* homework assignment?"

Coral and I flapped our wings.

Mom shook her head and laughed. "You really are going to be okay, aren't you?"

"Better than ever," I swore.

"I believe you." She brushed a kiss on my forehead before walking back to the picnic table, where she served cake to Coral's family.

I watched her and Mr. and Mrs. Ashby for a while.

"Think they'll be okay without us?" Coral asked.

"It'll be hard at first," I said, "but they'll make it. At least your parents still have your little brothers."

As if on cue, the boys started throwing cake at each other. "I don't know that having Aidan and Ian is a *good* thing." She turned to me. "When's Dan getting here?"

I looked at my watch. "Should be any time now. You won't be too far behind us, will you?"

"Naw, I'll be up a couple hours later." She lowered her sunglasses. "He's a good catch, Trin."

"Yeah," I agreed, a sappy smile on my face. "Who knew?"

"Kiri."

"That she did," I said thoughtfully.

"How's Dan's family doing with him leaving?"

I shrugged. "They're having a hard time. But I think Mr. Devlin has really turned around. I told you he quit his job, right? Well, yesterday he applied to work at the Miami-Dade State Attorney's Office, which is a MASSIVE pay cut."

"That's great." She looked at my sober face. "Isn't it?"

"I have mixed feelings, but then I figure if cons can find God, why can't Mr. Devlin earn redemption by locking up bad guys?"

"Right." She nodded. "At least he could accomplish something good. He wouldn't be able to do that in jail."

"It's a start anyhow. And boy did that come as a shock to Alan Kelley and Dr. Erskine."

"I bet!" Coral said with a smirk.

"But I think the best thing Mr. Devlin is doing is fixing things with Dan," I admitted.

"We all get a new beginning, don't we?" Coral asked.

I pulled my glass of iced tea out of the sand and held it aloft in a toast. *Tabula rasa.*

"Tabula rasa." Coral tapped her glass against mine and we both drank to our fresh slates.

"I'm going down to the water," I told Coral.

"You want to come?"

"Nope." She stood. "I'm going to have some cake before my brothers are wearing it all."

I walked to the water's edge and let the waves lap my toes. The sun was high, the sky a flawless blue. I took a few steps and then turned around to watch the ocean slowly erase my footprints. Each new foamy ripple smoothed away the impression I'd made.

Inevitably, I thought about Rafe. He'd left an imprint on me, but with each day, each new sunrise, the scar lightened.

One last swirl washed away the last of my tracks.

"Tabula rasa," I whispered.

Familiar, warm arms wrapped around my waist and I leaned back into the embrace.

"What are you doing?" Dan asked.

"Saying hello to a new beginning."

"Does that mean you're ready to go?" he asked.

I turned in his arms, hugging him back.

"It does." I caressed his cheek. "Are you?"

"Yep, all packed. But it was hard to say good-bye."

"I imagine knowing you're pre-law helped some."

Dan laughed. "Pretty soon there will be two Devlins locking up the bad guys."

"I feel safer already," I said, snuggling closer.

"I have something for you." He reached into his pocket, pulled out a small jewelry box, and flipped it open.

"Oh, Dan," I gasped. "It's gorgeous."

He pulled a delicate necklace from the box. The silver pendant had three sterling feathers dangling from a round hoop. A web was woven through the circle and a turquoise bead was caught in the strands.

"Turn around," he said.

I held up my hair so he could fasten it, then spun around to show him.

"Beautiful," he said, brushing my lips with a tender kiss. "So is the necklace."

"Thank you," I said, holding out the pendant so I could see it.

"It's a dream catcher," he said. "The Chippewa Indians believe the web catches bad dreams and good dreams pass through the hole in the center to the owner. When the sun rises the bad dreams caught in the web dissolve away."

"I love it." I took his hands in mine. "And I love you."

"I love you, too, Trin." He smoothed my wind-ruffled hair. "Let's get going. We've got a long trip ahead of us."

As we held hands and walked back to tell everyone good-bye, I realized something. Dreams aren't windows to the soul or doorways to the mind. They're reflections of the heart. And right now, my heart was starting a new journey.

I couldn't wait to see how my next book began.

Want more summer romance with a
deadly twist? Turn the page for an excerpt
of *Killer Cruise* by Jennifer Shaw

Chapter 1

Cute guys are my weakness.

I'll be the first to admit it.

As soon as I see one, I instantly go into flirt mode.

Today was no exception.

I was lying on a blue-and-white-striped chaise lounge, wearing the most adorable red-and-white polka-dot bikini. I knew I looked good and I could see guys staring at me from behind their mirrored sunglasses. It was hard *not* to notice. Some of them even lowered their sunglasses to get a better look.

If I were at the beach, I would just gather up my things and go home. Escape the temptation—that's what my boyfriend, Finn, would have wanted me to do.

But I was on a cruise ship, and everywhere

you looked there were cute guys. There was no escape!

So how could I *not* flirt?

For me, flirting is like breathing. It's just something I do.

I've never wondered why I like to flirt. It's part of being me, I guess. I want people to like me. I want them to see *me*—Ashley Bishop—and I don't think many people do. My father, unfortunately, is one of those people. It's hard being the daughter of a workaholic. But don't get me wrong—I know my father loves me. He just works really long hours overseeing his company, BPE—Bishop Pharmaceutical Enterprises—so he can give me, my mother, and my older half sister, Charlotte, everything we could possibly want.

This cruise is the perfect example.

My sixteenth birthday is at the end of the week. Instead of just throwing a birthday party, I asked my father if I could do something different. After all, sixteen is a *major* birthday. I didn't want something gross and over-the-top like those spoiled brats usually do on that MTV show *My Super Sweet 16*. I asked Daddy if I could take a cruise to the Bahamas and invite some of my closest friends.

He said yes.

Originally my parents were going to chaperone us, but then Daddy had to fly to Europe on business and my mother had her own job crisis going on. Because of previous commitments, none of the other parents were able to take their place, but luckily Daddy was good friends with the captain of the ship, who promised to have his staff keep an eye on us.

Anyway, as soon as Daddy gave me the green light, I got on the phone with my two best friends, Simone Greer and Kristine Fisher, and told them to start packing their bags. I knew from the start that my guest list would also have to include Tabitha Varvatos. Tabitha and I aren't exactly best friends, even though we've known each other since kindergarten, but our mothers are. I guess they've always hoped we'd be as close as they are, but we're not. Tabitha and I compete with each other for everything—grades, guys, clothes, and popularity. The list goes on and on. I guess you could call us frenemies. I hadn't wanted to invite Tabby—she *hates* it when I call her that, but the nickname *so* fits. She's exactly like a cat—sly and sneaky! But, as predicted, my mother insisted that I give sneaky Tabby a birthday cruise invite.

Of course, Charlotte was on my guest list too, and her boyfriend, Sam. They're both going to be seniors next month. I couldn't exactly celebrate my birthday without my half sister, and I was *determined* to make her have some fun. There's more to life than just studying for your SATs.

I also invited Finn O'Brien, my boyfriend. Finn is the guy that every girl at my high school wishes she could go out with. He's tall, blond, and blue-eyed, with a killer smile and two of the most adorable dimples you've ever seen. He plays tennis and rugby and volleyball and has that All-American look that you see in Abercrombie & Fitch ads. He's definitely a hottie. We've been going out since January. On the first day of class after our Christmas break, he asked if he could walk me home. I go to school in New York City on the Upper East Side, and I live only a few blocks from there. Anyway, instead of answering, I *slowly* squeezed his bicep and then started walking down the hallway and looking over my shoulder to make sure he was following. He was. Sometimes it's not what you say but what you do.

Finn's different from the other guys I've dated. For one thing, he's going to be a senior. Because he's older than me, he thinks he knows more than I do, which is totally annoying. He also likes being in charge—well, what guy doesn't?—and whenever we go out, he makes all the plans.

At first I didn't mind. After all, the guy usually does all the planning when you first start dating. Then, once you get to know each other—once you're a *couple*—you kind of take turns.

Not Finn.

He still calls all the shots.

Lately that's been bugging me too. I mean, Finn is really fun, but things haven't been perfect between us for a while.

"You're frowning," Simone said, breaking into my thoughts. "No frowning! We're on a cruise!"

I turned to where Simone was lying on a blue-and-white-striped chaise lounge of her own, applying coconut oil to her glistening brown skin, being careful not to get any on her tiny white bikini.

"Where did Finn disappear to?" Simone asked, capping the bottle of coconut oil.

"She's not thinking about Finn," Kristine said from the other chaise lounge, sitting up and pushing her huge sunglasses on top of her blond head. "She's been too busy staring at Smoothie Guy."

Simone propped herself up on an elbow. "Smoothie Guy?"

Kristine nodded. "That yummy piece of eye candy behind the juice bar."

I watched as Simone glanced in the direction Kristine was pointing. Her brown eyes instantly lit up.

"Yummy is right!" She ran her tongue over

the top of her cherry-coated lips. A look that I was *very* familiar with washed over her face. I like to call it her hunting look. "I think I might want a taste of that," she said bluntly.

The words slipped out of my mouth before I could stop them. "I saw him first!"

Simone and Kristine both turned to stare at me, completely shocked. I have to admit, I was a little shocked too.

"Don't you already have a boyfriend?" Simone asked.

"Do I? I haven't seen Finn since we got on board," I complained. "I think he's playing volleyball in the pool on the next deck."

Simone shrugged. "That's what happens when you date a jock. Been there, done that. Get used to it."

"You're not thinking of cheating on Finn?" Kristine asked.

"I'm not going to cheat on Finn," I told them. "And if I were going to cheat on him, I wouldn't do it when we're trapped together for a week. I'd only get caught."

"Then why are you so interested in Mr.

Smoothie?" Simone asked.

"I'm not."

"Are you sure?" she shot back, raising an eyebrow at me.

Simone can read my mind. We've been best friends since kindergarten and she's always known what I'm going to do, sometimes before I do.

"Yes, I'm sure I'm not interested," I answered her. "I'm just thirsty. I'm going to go get a smoothie. Does anyone want one?"

"I'm fine," Kristine said, flipping onto her stomach on her chaise lounge and opening a copy of *Cosmo*.

"I'm going to take a dip in the pool," Simone said, pulling her hair back into a ponytail. "There are some cute guys in the deep end. Since Smoothie Guy is off-limits, maybe I can get a date with one of them."

It was on the tip of my tongue to tell Simone that if she was interested in Smoothie Guy, I wouldn't stand in her way. But I didn't.

Besides, if she were really interested in him, I knew she would have made a play for him already. This wasn't the first time we'd fought over a guy.

But we *weren't* fighting over him. I was Finn's girlfriend. All I was doing was getting a smoothie.

When I got up to the juice bar, Smoothie Guy gave me a dazzling smile. "What'll it be?"

I pretended to read the menu while I secretly checked him out. He was busy rinsing out a blender, so he didn't notice that my eyes were more focused on him than the drink selection.

In terms of looks, he was the complete opposite of Finn, with tousled black curls and light gray eyes. *Dazzling smile*—but I already mentioned that. He was wearing a white tank top, which showed off his taut chest and muscular arms, and a pair of khaki shorts that exposed his well-developed calves. He looked like a swimmer—lean but strong.

"Make up your mind?" he asked, catching me off-guard.

"I'll have a strawberry smoothie," I said quickly, hoping he hadn't caught me ogling him.

I watched as he threw strawberries and ice cubes into a blender, then added some milk. As he worked, I tried to think of something to say, but my mind was a blank. Where had my powers of flirtation gone?

"One strawberry smoothie," he said, placing the frothy drink in front of me.

I handed him my card key so he could charge the smoothie to my cabin and then popped a straw into my drink, slowly taking a sip. I'd reapplied some lip gloss before walking over, so I knew my lips looked shiny and slick.

"How's it taste?" he asked. "Good?"

I took another sip. "Very good. Best smoothie I've ever had. But I'm not surprised."

"You're not? How come?"

"I'll bet you're good at everything you do."

Success! My flirting powers were back.

"They're not hard to make. You just throw all the ingredients into a blender and press a button."

"The last time I tried that, our kitchen ceiling was splattered with vanilla milk shake."

"Don't tell me," he laughed. "You forgot to

press down on the blender lid?"

I nodded. "Uh-huh. Kitchens and I don't mesh well together. I can't even boil water."

"You can't be that bad."

"Want to bet? Last Father's Day I tried to make my father *frozen* waffles and I *burned* them!"

"You probably forgot to turn down the setting on the toaster. It could happen to anyone."

"You're sweet," I said, taking another sip of my smoothie. "Have you been making these very long?"

He shrugged as he wiped down the counter with a white towel. "Two years. I work during the summers and whenever I have breaks from school."

"What's your name?" I asked.

"Logan Gallo. Yours?"

"Ashley Bishop."

"Welcome aboard."

"This your first cruise?"

"Yep."

Logan leaned across the counter toward me. "Well, let me give you a tip then. Avoid the nightclub on the Panama Deck. The best music is in Club Paradise. That's on the Diablo Deck. The Club Paradise d.j. is great."

"You like to dance?" I asked.

"It depends who I'm with. If I'm hanging out with the guys, I'll just listen. But if I'm with a girl, I'll pull her out onto the dance floor."

"When was the last time you went dancing?" I asked. The question popped out before I could stop it!

"It's been a while, but who knows?" He gazed at me. "I might feel like dancing this week."

"If I stop by Club Paradise, I'll look for you," I said, hoping he would be there tonight.

"I'll do the same."

"Okay." I started walking away and then turned around. Again, the words popped out before I could stop them. "I'm having a birthday party on Saturday night. It's for my Sweet Sixteen. Want to come?"

He paused for a second and I almost thought he was going to blow me off. But then he gave me a smile and said, "Sure. I'd love to come." After that, a customer came up behind me and ordered a tropical smoothie. Logan and I said good-bye and he got busy chopping a pineapple.

As I walked away, I asked myself why I had invited Logan, someone I barely knew, to my party. But I couldn't explain it. Besides, what was the big deal? Over the years I'd thrown lots of parties where I invited people I barely knew. I told myself that this was no different. I'd probably make some other new friends on the cruise and invite them, too.

When I got back to the pool, I saw that Simone's and Kristine's chaise lounges were empty, and neither one was in the water.

My stomach grumbled, letting me know it was lunchtime. I was in the mood for some cheese fries at the Burger Shack, but before looking for the girls and getting something to eat, I decided to head back to my room. I'd finished my bottle of sunblock and I needed to get another. It was a scorcher of a day and the last thing I wanted was to look like a lobster after one day of vacation.

Once I was back inside the ship, the icy coldness of the air-conditioning cooled me off. Of course, I was only wearing my tiny two-piece and flip-flops. As I walked down the hallway to my room, I couldn't help but notice how deserted it was. Everyone must have been having lunch.

As I kept walking, I heard footsteps behind me. I turned to see if it was Simone or Kristine, but no one was there. Weird. I turned back around and kept walking, sipping on my smoothie. But then, as I got closer to my room, the lights in the hallway began flickering, casting shadows on the walls.

The footsteps started up again, and they were getting closer.

And closer.

I should have turned around, but I didn't. I pulled out my card key and began walking faster.

So did the person behind me.

I knew my imagination was probably playing tricks on me and that I should just look over my shoulder, but I couldn't. All I wanted was to

14

get inside my room.

When I finally reached my cabin I fumbled to insert my card key and sighed with relief when I heard the lock click open.

As I opened the door, I felt a shove. I fell to the floor of my room, dropping what was left of my smoothie as I heard the door slam shut behind me.

When I turned onto my back, I gasped.

Standing above me was a figure wearing a black stocking mask.